Mrs. Noodlekugel and Four Blind Mice

To Jill, of course
D. P.

For Terry, Zita, and Harvey
A. S.

Mrs. Noodlekugel
AND Four Blind Mice

Daniel Pinkwater

illustrated by
Adam Stower

CANDLEWICK PRESS

Text copyright © 2013 by Daniel Pinkwater
Illustrations copyright © 2013 by Adam Stower

First edition 2013

Library of Congress Catalog Card Number 2012947756
ISBN 978-0-7636-5054-4

13 14 15 16 17 18 BVG 10 9 8 7 6 5 4 3 2 1

Printed in Berryville, VA, U.S.A.

This book was typeset in Esprit.
The illustrations were done in ink.

Candlewick Press
99 Dover Street
Somerville, Massachusetts 02144

visit us at www.candlewick.com

Chapter
1

Mrs. Noodlekugel's little house was in a sort of backyard behind a tall apartment building. The house was built long before the apartment buildings that had grown up all around it. Mrs. Noodlekugel lived with her cat, Mr. Fuzzface, and four fat mice. Nick and Maxine, a human boy and girl, brother and sister, lived in one of the apartment buildings. They discovered the hidden backyard and the little house, and Mrs. Noodlekugel, and became friends.

Mrs. Noodlekugel also became the children's babysitter. They would visit her in the little house when their parents were away, and sometimes when they were not. Very often, they would have tea and cookies with Mrs. Noodlekugel, Mr. Fuzzface, and the mice.

One day, the mice were making a terrible mess, spreading cookie crumbs everywhere, and spilling tea.

"The mice are becoming very far-sighted," Mrs. Noodlekugel said. "It is not that they have bad table manners, just that they do not see very well. There is nothing to do but take them downtown and have them fitted with eyeglasses."

"I was thinking the same," said Mr. Fuzzface, Mrs. Noodlekugel's cat.

"We will take them tomorrow," Mrs. Noodlekugel said. "Children, would you like to come along? We will go on the bus. You can help us, and it will be interesting."

"You want us to come with you on the bus?" Nick and Maxine asked.

"If you don't mind," Mrs. Noodlekugel said. "Mr. Fuzzface has to go in
a cat carrier — it is a rule of the bus

company. I have such a cat carrier. I will ask Mike the janitor to get it from the attic. Then you children could help me carry him."

Mike the janitor mopped the floors and carried out the garbage and fixed things around the apartment building. Sometimes he also helped Mrs. Noodle-kugel. Nick and Maxine knew him. He had a blue chin and a mustache like a brush, and liked to sit in a little room in the basement, eating stewed tomatoes out of a can, talking to himself and listening to the radio.

"We will have to ask our parents," Nick and Maxine said.

"I am sure they will agree," Mrs. Noodlekugel said. "It is a perfectly respectable bus company."

Chapter 2

Nick and Maxine turned up at Mrs. Noodlekugel's house in the morning with a note from their parents saying they could go. Mrs. Noodlekugel had on her coat and a hat with flowers and plastic cherries. She was trying to coax Mr. Fuzzface into a cat carrier, which

was like a big handbag with a little screened window.

"It is wrong to make me ride in that thing," Mr. Fuzzface said.

"It is only for a little while," Mrs. Noodlekugel said. "And it is a rule of the bus company."

"I object to being treated like an animal," Mr. Fuzzface said.

"I understand," Mrs. Noodlekugel said.

"It is undignified," Mr. Fuzzface said.

"It is," Mrs. Noodlekugel said.

"I protest," Mr. Fuzzface said.

"But you want to come along," Mrs. Noodlekugel said. "You want to come downtown with the children and the mice and me, do you not?"

"Yes."

"And you want to visit the oculist, so the mice can be fitted with eyeglasses, and afterward we will go and have something nice to eat. You would like that, wouldn't you?"

"May I order anything I want?" Mr. Fuzzface asked.

"Of course," Mrs. Noodlekugel said.

"Ice cream and sardines?" Mr. Fuzzface asked.

"If you want," Mrs. Noodlekugel said.

"I will ride in the cat carrier," Mr. Fuzzface said. "But it is wrong."

"It is this way every time we go anywhere," Mrs. Noodlekugel said to Nick and Maxine.

"But where are the mice?" Nick asked.

"Oh, I did not forget the mice," Mrs. Noodlekugel said. "Look closely at my hat."

Nick and Maxine looked closely at Mrs. Noodlekugel's hat. Among the plastic cherries and flowers, the four mice were attached to the hat by elastic bands around their middles.

"They are quite safe and secure," Mrs. Noodlekugel said.

"The mice get to look out the windows of the bus," Mr. Fuzzface said from inside the cat carrier. "They do not have to ride in a stuffy cat carrier. Why can't I ride on your hat?"

"You are too big to ride on my hat," Mrs. Noodlekugel said. "Now let us go and wait for the bus."

Chapter
3

Mrs. Noodlekugel and the children waited for the bus. When the bus came, she said to the driver, "One grown-up, two children, and a cat."

"Full fare for the adult, half fare for the children, fifteen cents for the cat," the driver said.

"There are mice on my hat," Mrs. Noodlekugel said.

"No charge for mice on hats," the driver said. "Do not let them run loose."

"Of course not," Mrs. Noodlekugel said. "Come, children, let's move back in the bus and take seats."

Nick and Maxine took a seat with Mr. Fuzzface in the cat carrier between them.

Mrs. Noodlekugel sat in the seat behind them. The mice looked out the bus window, and Mr. Fuzzface told a story.

"I was a railroad cat. I would ride with the engineer. At night I would sit on the engineer's shoulder and look ahead for obstacles on the tracks, because cats, as you know, have excellent night vision. During the day I would sleep in the engineer's hat.

The railroad men fed me ham sandwiches and pickles. I was famous up and down the railroad.

"I was the one who prevented a train wreck on the Poughkeepsie railroad bridge. The signal had gone out, and I sat on the track blinking one eye, and then the other. Cats' eyes shine in the dark, as you know, and when my eyes were picked up in the headlights of the oncoming train, the brave

engineer brought it to a stop
and saved many lives.
The president of the
railroad gave me a
gold medal, which,
as you can see, I wear
on my collar to this
day. Mrs. Noodlekugel
has one just like it."

"Mrs. Noodlekugel does?"

"Yes, Mrs. Noodlekugel was the
engineer driving that train. It was how
we met."

Nick asked, "Mrs. Noodlekugel, you
were a railroad engineer?"

"Oh, yes, I was the only lady engineer for many years. And Mr. Fuzzface was a famous railroad cat."

"My father, Oldface, was a railroad cat, too," Mr. Fuzzface said. "He was the engineer's cat on Old 97, on the Lynchburg-to-Danville run. I don't remember him very well, but my mother, Momface, told me stories about him. One night he disappeared. We looked for him everywhere. I still look for him — a long and skinny yellow cat with one ragged ear and a squinty eye. It is my greatest wish to find my long-lost daddy."

"You want to find him because you miss him so much," Maxine said.

"He left my mother to raise seven kittens all by herself," Mr. Fuzzface said. "I want to bite him. If I ever run into him, I will teach him a lesson."

"Now, Mr. Fuzzface," Mrs. Noodle-kugel said, "perhaps Oldface had a reason for disappearing. You know, it's a mighty hard road from Lynchburg to Danville, and you have to make a three-mile grade."

"I will give him ten seconds to explain," Mr. Fuzzface said. "After that I will be all over him like sardines on ice cream."

Chapter 4

Let us get off the bus," Mrs. Noodle-kugel said. "We are downtown, and we have arrived."

Mrs. Noodlekugel, with the four mice on her hat, and Nick and Maxine, carrying Mr. Fuzzface in the cat carrier, got off the bus.

"Look! There is the oculist's!" Mrs. Noodlekugel said. "Let us go in."

The oculist's shop was full of shiny glass cases. In the cases were pairs of shiny eyeglasses. There were strange-looking machines and a special chair to sit in while being examined.

"Hello, Mrs. Noodlekugel," Dr. Bril, the oculist, said. "Hello, children. And I see you have brought Mr. Fuzzface. Hello, cat. What may I do for you all today?"

"These mice on my hat need their eyes examined," Mrs. Noodlekugel said.

"Ah, mice," Dr. Bril said. "I will need to stack some books on the seat of my special examination chair so they will be high enough."

Dr. Bril carried thick books and stacked them on the seat of the special examination chair. Mrs. Noodlekugel

helped the mice get out of the elastic
bands that held them to her hat and
helped the first mouse get to the top of
the stack of books.

"The mice cannot read, of course," Dr. Bril said.

"No, they are mice," Mrs. Noodle-kugel said.

"Ordinarily, we test vision with an eye chart," Dr. Bril said. "It has large letters at the top, smaller letters underneath, and still smaller letters underneath those, and so on until the letters are very small. But that would not do with these mice."

"No, it would not," Mrs. Noodle-kugel said.

"So, I will use this special eye chart, made for mice," Dr. Bril said. "As you see, there is a picture of a mouse in a cowboy hat, a cat, and a piece of cheese at the top, quite large. Beneath that is a picture of a piece of cheese, a cat, and a mouse in a cowboy hat, somewhat smaller. The next line has a picture of a cat, a mouse in a cowboy hat, and a piece of cheese, smaller yet, and so on. I will point to each picture, and the mouse will tell me what it sees."

"The mice cannot talk, either," Mrs. Noodlekugel said.

"Well, we will do our best," Dr. Bril said. He pointed to the largest picture of a mouse in a cowboy hat. The mouse on top of the stack of books clapped its paws and jumped up and down.

Then Dr. Bril pointed to the largest picture of a cat. The mouse stroked its whiskers.

He pointed to the largest picture of a piece of cheese, and the mouse rubbed its belly.

"This is satisfactory," Dr. Bril said. "We will continue." He pointed to the pictures on the next line, and the line after that. The mouse clapped its paws, stroked its whiskers, and rubbed its belly.

This continued, until when Dr. Bril pointed to a picture, the mouse became confused and scratched its head. Then Dr. Bril made a note on a little card.

"This mouse has musopia," Dr. Bril said. "We can fit eyeglasses for that. Now let us test the next mouse."

When he had tested all the mice, Dr. Bril said, "I will go into the back room and make the eyeglasses. Please wait here. You may read magazines and look at the pictures on the walls."

Chapter 5

After a little while, Dr. Bril came out of the back room with four tiny pairs of eyeglasses. "I have chosen frames in red, yellow, blue, and green so the mice will not get their eyeglasses mixed up." He carefully put a pair of eyeglasses on each mouse.

The mice peered through their new eyeglasses. They looked at each other, and at the pictures on the walls. They looked all around the oculist's shop. They turned this way and that, faster and faster. They squeaked excitedly.

They then began to scurry. They scurried all around the shop. They climbed the shelves, got on top of tables and chairs, peered out the shop window, spun until they were dizzy, and danced in a circle.

"The mice appear to be happy with their new eyeglasses," Mrs. Noodlekugel said.

"Yes, they are seeing much better," Dr. Bril said. "They are enjoying it."

Mrs. Noodlekugel thanked Dr. Bril. Dr. Bril said good-bye to the mice, gave lollipops in the shape of eyeglasses to Nick and Maxine, and patted Mr. Fuzzface on the head.

Chapter 6

The mice struggled and kicked and refused to ride attached to Mrs. Noodlekugel's hat with elastic bands. They wanted to walk on the sidewalk. So did Mr. Fuzzface.

"You must hold paws and stay together," Mrs. Noodlekugel told the mice. "And on the bus going home, you must ride on my hat."

Nick and Maxine heard a tiny gurgling noise. "What is that?" they asked.

"It is the mice," Mrs. Noodlekugel said. "Their tummies are rumbling. They are hungry."

"So am I," Mr. Fuzzface said. "Are we going to a restaurant?"

"Yes. We will walk along until we find one," Mrs. Noodlekugel said.

So they walked along, Mrs. Noodle-kugel leading the way, Nick and Maxine carrying Mr. Fuzzface's empty cat carrier, the mice holding paws and looking all around through their new eyeglasses, with Mr. Fuzzface following behind, making sure the mice got into no trouble.

"Stay together," Mrs. Noodlekugel said. "We are looking for a nice restaurant."

They came to a place with a sign over the door: DIRTY SALLY'S LUNCHROOM.

"Here is a nice place," Mrs. Noodle-kugel said.

"Dirty Sally's Lunchroom?" Nick asked.

"It doesn't have a very nice name," Maxine said.

"I am sure it is nice," Mrs. Noodle-kugel said. "Only a good restaurant would have a disgusting name like that. They must call it that to discourage the timid. We can go in."

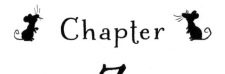

Chapter 7

In Dirty Sally's Lunchroom, none of the chairs matched, and the tables wobbled. The walls were painted pea green, and the floor was covered with yellow linoleum that was old and scuffed. There was a counter at one side of the room where some old men were eating Nesselrode pie.

"Oh, it is charming!" Mrs. Noodle-kugel said. "Let us sit at a table and decide what we want to order."

They sat at a table, which wobbled.

"Look!" Maxine whispered. "The waiter is a monkey!"

Mrs. Noodlekugel turned and looked. "So he is. He is quite tall for a monkey."

The monkey waiter came to the table carrying a tray with glasses of water. He put a glass of water before Mrs. Noodlekugel, Maxine, and Nick and a saucer of water in front of Mr. Fuzzface. He saw the mice and brought tiny cups of water for them. Then he put a card on the table. Printed on the card was, *Tell the monkey what you want.*

"I suppose the monkey cannot speak," Mrs. Noodlekugel said.

"I would like ice cream with sardines on top," Mr. Fuzzface said.

The monkey held up a card that read, *We don't have that.*

"Do you have ice cream?" Mrs. Noodlekugel asked.

The monkey held up a card that read, *YES.*

"Do you have sardines?"

The monkey held up a card that read, *NO.*

"Mr. Fuzzface, they have ice cream, but they do not have sardines," Mrs. Noodlekugel said. "Would you like ice cream without sardines?"

"Absolutely not," Mr. Fuzzface said. "There is no point in eating ice cream without sardines."

"Perhaps you will allow me to order for us all," Mrs. Noodlekugel said. To the waiter she said, "Do you have cheesecake?"

The monkey held up a card that read:

Try Dirty Sally's
FAMOUS
CHEESECAKE

"We will have four pieces of cheese-cake," Mrs. Noodlekugel said. "And one piece of cheesecake cut into four for the mice. And tea. We will have tea."

The monkey nodded and went away.

"Cheesecake? What is cheesecake?" Maxine and Nick asked. "It sounds awful. Does it have Swiss cheese? Does it have cheddar cheese?"

"It is made with cream cheese," Mrs. Noodlekugel said. "It is very nice, and you will like it."

The monkey waiter brought four big pieces of cheesecake, one piece of cheesecake cut into four for the mice, a pot of tea, and cups. Even cut into four, the pieces of cheesecake were as big as the mice. The mice sniffed, tasted, and rubbed their bellies. Nick and Maxine tasted their cheesecake.

"Yum," Nick said.

"Yum," Maxine said.

"This would be even better with sardines," Mr. Fuzzface said.

Chapter 8

Mrs. Noodlekugel poured tea and took dainty forkfuls of cheesecake. Nick and Maxine ate their cheesecake, *nom, nom, nom.* Mr. Fuzzface lapped his cheesecake. The mice nibbled for all they were worth.

"Yum!"

Nom!

Lap!

Nibble, nibble, nibble!

There was more cheesecake than any of them could finish. One by one, the children, Mr. Fuzzface, and Mrs. Noodlekugel sat back in their chairs to rest and wonder if they could eat

another bite. The mice kept nibbling for all they were worth.

Then the mice began to switch their tails and bounce up and down. They pulled off chunks of cheesecake and threw them at one another. They squeaked and spun in circles, chasing their tails, and rolled on their backs, waving their tiny paws in the air.

"Mrs. Noodlekugel, the mice are behaving strangely," Maxine said.

"They are acting crazy," Nick said.

"They have eaten too much cheese-cake," Mrs. Noodlekugel said. "It is going to their heads."

"It is the sugar," Mr. Fuzzface said. "They are not used to so much."

The mice climbed down the table leg and began to scurry all around Dirty Sally's Lunchroom. An old man came in to get some Nesselrode pie, and when he opened the door, the mice scurried out.

"Oh, my!" Mrs. Noodlekugel said. "The mice have gone outside! Come, children! Come, Mr. Fuzzface! We must go after them!" To the monkey waiter, she called, "We will come back! Do not take away our cheesecake!" And to the children and the cat, she called, "Let us hurry! We must collect the mice before they get into trouble!"

Chapter 9

Outside in the street, cars, trucks, and buses rumbled past. The sidewalk was crowded with people walking.

"Do you see the mice?" Mrs. Noodle-kugel asked. "Look for the mice!"

The children and Mr. Fuzzface walked up and down, calling the mice.

"Here, mice!" they called. "Nice mousie, mousie, mousie! Where are you, mice?"

There was not a mouse to be seen.

A policeman came along. "We are looking for four runaway mice," Mrs. Noodlekugel told the policeman.

"Where did you see them last?" the policeman asked.

"Just here," Mrs. Noodlekugel said. "They ran out of the restaurant."

"Can you describe the mice?" the policeman asked.

"They are mice," Mrs. Noodlekugel said. "They are gray. They are small. There are four of them."

"What are their names?" the policeman asked.

"We just call them mice," Mrs. Noodlekugel said. "We do not know their names."

"I will help you look for them," the

policeman said. He began to walk up and down, looking for the mice. "Here, mice!" he called. "Nice mousie, mousie, mousie! Where are you, mice?"

There was not a mouse to be seen.

They came to a narrow space, an alley between two buildings.

"Let us look here," Mrs. Noodle-kugel said.

In the alley, they saw four mice sitting on the lid of a garbage can. With them, on top of the garbage can, was a long and skinny yellow cat with one ragged ear and a squinty eye.

"Is dese your mices?" the cat said.

"Yes!" Mrs. Noodlekugel said. "Naughty mice! Why did you run away?"

The mice looked down at their feet and played with their whiskers nervously.

"Saw dese mices," the yellow cat said. "Mices not belong here. Told them sit still. Then think what do with mices. Then you come."

"So these are the mice?" the policeman asked.

"Yes, they are naughty mice," Mrs. Noodlekugel said.

"I am glad you found them," the
policeman said. "I will be going now."

"Thank you for helping us look
for the mice," Mrs. Noodlekugel said.
"Will you join us for a cup of tea and
a piece of cheesecake at Dirty Sally's?"

"Thank you," said the policeman.
"May I have Nesselrode pie instead?"

"Of course," Mrs. Noodlekugel said. And to the yellow cat, she said, "We would like to thank you for taking care of the mice. Please join us, too."

"Want ice cream with sardines," the yellow cat said.

"They have no sardines," Mr. Fuzzface said. "But the cheesecake is good."

"OK," said the yellow cat.

Chapter 10

Mrs. Noodlekugel, Nick and Maxine, Mr. Fuzzface, the four mice, the policeman, and the yellow cat were seated around the wobbly table.

"Please take the mice's cheesecake away," Mrs. Noodlekugel told the monkey waiter. "They have had enough. And please bring Nesselrode pie for the policeman and a piece of cheesecake for the yellow cat. They are our guests."

"Dis is nice," said the yellow cat.

"We were noticing that you can talk," Maxine said to the yellow cat.

"I noticed that, too," said the policeman.

"But you talk differently from me," Mr. Fuzzface said. "I was taught to speak by Mrs. Noodlekugel."

"Was learned to talk by rough sailor-men," the yellow cat said. "Probably why not talk nice like you."

"Are you an offshore kitty?" Mrs. Noodlekugel asked.

"First was railroad cat," the yellow cat said.

"I was a railroad cat," Mr. Fuzzface said. "And my father was a railroad cat."

"Took train to San Francisco," the yellow cat said. "In San Francisco, taken aboard big ship. Ship went away for years and years. Not able to write. Besides, didn't know anybody able to read. So can't send letter. Must have been like disappeared."

"My father disappeared," Mr. Fuzz-face said.

"Left seven kittens behind," the yellow cat said.

"I was one of seven kittens who were left behind," Mr. Fuzzface said.

"When finally came back, kittens gone, don't know where. Mate gone, don't know where."

"My mother went I don't know where," Mr. Fuzzface said.

"Mate was called Momface," the yellow cat said.

"My mother was called Momface," Mr. Fuzzface said.

The yellow cat looked at Mr. Fuzz-face with his eye that was not squinty. "What your name?"

"My name is Mr. Fuzzface," Mr. Fuzzface said.

"Fuzzface, I yam yer fadder."

Chapter
11

Oldface?" Mr. Fuzzface asked.

"Oldface," the yellow cat said.

The two cats stared at each other across the table, Mr. Fuzzface with both eyes and Oldface with his good eye. No one said anything.

Nick and Maxine wondered if Mr. Fuzzface was going to bite his father, as he had said he would . . . but he didn't.

"I call this a remarkable coincidence," Mrs. Noodlekugel said.

"So do I," said the policeman, whose name was Officer Chestnut.

"And where do you live now, Mr. Oldface?" Mrs. Noodlekugel asked.

"Alley, where mices was, where you met," Oldface said.

"And is it satisfactory?" Mrs. Noodlekugel asked Oldface.

"Is alley," Oldface said. "Is wet when rains, is cold when snows."

"I was thinking, would you prefer to live in a little house, where it is dry when it rains and warm when it snows and there is plenty to eat?"

"You crazy, lady? Who wouldn't prefer?" Oldface said.

"Of course, there is the problem of the bus. We have only one cat carrier."

"I can arrange a ride in a police car," Officer Chestnut said.

"Oooh!" said Nick and Maxine.

"And of course, we have to ask Mr. Fuzzface," Mrs. Noodlekugel said. "Mr. Fuzzface, is it all right with you if Oldface comes and stays with us?"

"Of course it is all right," Mr. Fuzzface said. "He is my fadder."

Praise for *The Shadow Thief*

'Clearly [Adornetto] is already an Australian
literary phenomenon ... to read *The Shadow
Thief* is to be thrust into a fast-moving plot full
of menace and thrills, amply seeded with a
magnificently precocious vocabulary.'
The Courier-Mail

'... an impressive debut ... a wonderful fantasy
story, full of adventure and scary,
dark shadows.'
The Australian Women's Weekly

'... a fantastic achievement ...'
The Sunday Age

'... a comic fantasy full of magic.'
The Sydney Morning Herald

'You will be hooked by Alex's sparkling
dialogue and witty perceptive insights ...'
The Toowoomba Chronicle

Von Gobstopper's Arcade

Alexandra Adornetto

Angus&Robertson

Angus & Robertson
An imprint of HarperCollins*Publishers*, Australia

First published in Australia in 2009
by HarperCollins*Publishers* Australia Pty Ltd
ABN 36 009 913 517
www.harpercollins.com.au

HarperCollins*Publishers*
25 Ryde Road, Pymble, Sydney NSW 2073, Australia
31 View Road, Glenfield, Auckland 0627, New Zealand
1–A, Hamilton House, Connaught Place, New Delhi – 110 001, India
77–85 Fulham Palace Road, London W6 8JB, United Kingdom
2 Bloor Street East, 20th floor, Toronto, Ontario M4W 1A8, Canada
10 East 53rd Street, New York NY 10022, USA

National Library of Australia Cataloguing-in-Publication data:

Adornetto, Alexandra.
Vongobstopper's arcade / author, Alexandra Adornetto.
ISBN: 978 0 7322 8663 7 (hbk.)
Adornetto, Alexandra. Strangest adventures ; bk. 3.
For primary school age.
A823.4

Cover design and illustrations © Jenny Grigg 2009
Internal illustrations and design © Jenny Grigg 2009
Typeset in Adobe CaslonPro 12/16pt by Helen Beard, ECJ Aust Pty Ltd
Printed and bound in Australia by Griffin Press

70gsm Bulky Book Ivory used by HarperCollins*Publishers* is a natural, recyclable
product made from wood grown in sustainable forests. The manufacturing processes
conform to the environmental regulations in the country of origin, Finland.

5 4 3 2 1   09 10 11 12 13

To my mother, Grace, and my Aunt Ida for their ceaseless devotion, without which none of this would have happened.

Contents

Continued

'Peter,' said Wendy the comforter, 'I should love you in a beard'; and Mrs Darling stretched out her arms to him, but he repulsed her.

'Keep back, lady, no one is going to catch me and make me a man.'

Peter Pan and Wendy
J.M. Barrie

Prologue

The old wizard curled a withered hand into a fist, the bones visible through bluish skin. His lustreless eyes had difficulty focusing and his face twitched in anticipation. In his weakened state it was a struggle for him to keep himself upright in his chair and his breath came in spasms. The windowless room he sat in was cramped and lit only by dim candlelight.

The door was opened by a lithe young woman carrying a goblet filled with a congealed liquid the colour of calf's liver. She set the goblet down before the old man and heard him groan in relief.

'Drink, Master,' she urged, 'and your strength will return.'

The wizard grasped the cup in both hands

and downed its contents in a single gulp. Some colour returned to his cheeks as he looked vacantly at his attendant and wiped away the trickle dribbling down his chin. He sat up straighter and waited for his breathing to become more regular. He stretched out an arm from the elbow, as if testing it for renewed strength.

'I have been too rash,' the old man said. 'In my eagerness for victory I left holes in my plans, holes large enough for the enemy to slip through, again.' He laughed bitterly at some private recollection. 'We both know I cannot sustain another failure. The next strike must be infallible.'

'You cannot fail, Master,' breathed the woman, her cheeks flushed with excitement. When the old man beckoned to her she moved swiftly to kneel by his side. He whispered into her ear and her eyes closed in an expression of rapture.

'It is inspired!' the young woman cried, almost moved to tears by what she had heard. 'Pure genius.'

Pleased with the response, Lord Aldor's eyes lit up and his face twisted into a crazed smile.

Part I

A Place Called Home

CHAPTER ONE

Safety First

s children, we sometimes inhabit imaginary worlds where some of our best friends are inanimate playthings better known as toys. Do you have a favourite? I certainly do. His name is Lavender Ted and he has been my faithful sleeping companion ever since we became acquainted on my tenth birthday in 2003. He was given to me by my BFF (Best Friend Forever), Hailey, who has since moved to another city. Lavender Ted, as you may have already guessed, smells deliciously of lavender. That is hardly surprising as he is stuffed full of dried lavender seeds. It is a very comforting smell when you are trying to drift off to sleep.

Lavender Ted and I share a history. After our initial, instant connection I insisted he accompany us everywhere, including the occasional holiday to other continents. It is a habit I have struggled to outgrow. Somehow, I am not able to enjoy myself knowing that Lavender Ted is home alone when he might be soaking up the sun and sea air or feasting his eyes on the magnificent architecture that came out of Renaissance Venice. After all, it seems to me just as important for a bear to be well-travelled as it is for a child.

Lavender Ted is indeed a special favourite, but he is not the only toy whose comfort and wellbeing I felt personally responsible for whilst growing up. There was Molly, an almost-bald doll in checked overalls who was always a little bit rough and tumble. She used to enjoy riding on my tricycle and we often went on trips together to the bottom of the garden after packing a picnic lunch of fairy bread and frozen pineapple rings. There was bib-wearing Chocolate Bunny, so named because of his colour as well as his addiction to anything containing cocoa, and Tick-Tock Rabbit with

4

his immaculate green waistcoat, fob watch and constantly anxious expression. Then there was a quartet of porcelain dolls, Ally, Buttercup-Daisy, Lizzie and Polly, who formed a rather elite girls' club. It was impossible not to be seduced by their glossy curls, perfect features and satin frocks and stockings. I also had an odd and shameless attachment to a box full of marbles. For a while (and to my mother's consternation) I played with them almost every day; petting and scolding them as well as encouraging some friendly competition between them, for, as we children know, a little competition can bring out the best in us and is nowhere near as destructive as some experts would have us believe.

The point I am trying to make through all of this rambling is that toys are often a child's closest companions. These ties are not easily broken, even by well-intentioned adults in a hurry to see us grow up and move on to more useful endeavours. Toys never abandon us, even if we abandon them. Some children (As I have seen my own friends do) pack away their toys when they feel they have outgrown them, stuffing them in the backs of cupboards to gather dust. These children do not realise they are rejecting the most loyal friends they may ever have. If you are frowning now because you recognise that you fall into this category, do not despair. Fortunately, toys do not hold grudges, and once you realise the error of your ways and make amends they will welcome you back with open arms and never hold your previous unkindness against you.

I suppose by now you must be wondering where this preamble is leading and why on earth I have chosen to harangue you about the importance of toys and the pivotal role they play in our early lives. You may have guessed that this story is about several remarkable toys, to whom you will soon be introduced. At this point, however, I think it is high time we dropped in on the town of Drabville to check on its resilient occupants. I call Drabvillians *resilient* because, as you may recall, the town's courage has been tested more than once by the scheming of a mad magician who should have been planning how best to spend his twilight years rather than wreaking havoc on the innocent. Twice already the dauntless children of Drabville, led by Millipop Klompet and Ernest Perriclof, had defeated this oppressor.

The first time, Lord Aldor masterminded an insidious plot to steal the town's shadows. After his fiendishness was exposed and he was forced to beat a humiliating retreat, Drabvillians embraced life with a new vigour. Suddenly, being a Drabvillian actually *meant* something. It came to be associated with noble attitudes and behaviours, such as striving for freedom, fighting oppression and the use of ingenuity to overcome obstacles.

Then, as suddenly as it had sprung up, the town's euphoria dissolved one afternoon with the abduction of its children. It took very little time for the realisation to dawn that Lord Aldor had returned. The intriguing and fascinating Lampo Circus was a front for his revenge on the citizens of Drabville, its lavish big top tent swooping up their children and whisking them off to become pawns in Aldor's plot to destroy Queen Fidelis and her Fairy realm of Mirth. In their shock and horror the people of Drabville were quick to apportion blame. Fathers blamed mothers for not being more intuitive, and mothers blamed fathers for not being more authoritative. Everyone blamed the Bureau of Healthy Diversions for failing to check the credentials of the circus. The truth was, it had happened under their very noses and they had all been too preoccupied with celebration and self-expression to notice the danger. They were the adults and their primary duty was to protect their offspring. Instead they had delivered them with smiling faces into the hands of a villain.

Then one sunny afternoon, as mysteriously as they had vanished, the children returned. They were spotted by a local farmer, Shovèl Oats, as he ploughed his fields, sitting somewhat dazedly in the exact spot where the infamous Lampo Circus had once set up camp. The children's defeat of Lord Aldor for a second time was received with more reservation. The adults' overwhelming relief at seeing their children safely returned was tempered by caution. How could Drabville ensure that something this wicked never occurred again? The town decided to make security its first priority. They would not be caught off-guard

8

again. They would not fail their children a second time.

Measures were put in place which, although stifling at times, were designed to ensure the safety of all children. Firstly, a public awareness campaign encouraged citizens to report immediately the sighting of any suspicious characters or objects that could in any way compromise child safety. Reaction from some quarters was ridiculous. Let me give you some examples. In those early days after the children's return, a special voluntary group was set up called Protectors of the Safety and Security of Minors (POSSOM). On more than one occasion its members, wearing their possum-shaped berets and armed with rolling pins (batons being in short supply), were called out in the middle of the night because someone had found a spider with a malicious glint in its eye in their parlour, or heard strange laughter coming from their garden. Even an unattended shopping trolley filled with too many treats for responsible parenting was suddenly enough to raise the alarm. 'Better call POSSOM,' someone would suggest, and within minutes members of this organisation were immediately at the scene, examining the trolley's contents and blocking access to the aisles with giant yellow tape. Sometimes it would be hours before the all clear was given. Another thing that happened was the reform of the regulations surrounding the sale of confectionery. Every chocolate bar, lollipop or bag of sweets had to bear an official seal (a naked cherub blowing a trumpet) indicating that it had first been tested on a team of adult volunteers with no deleterious effects. Lastly, those in positions of responsibility with regard to the care of children had to reapply for their jobs. A full working knowledge of nursery rhymes as well as proven alertness in a crisis were suddenly highly desirable qualifications for anyone seeking re-employment.

Lord Aldor's return and his near success in abducting the children had dealt a serious blow to Drabville's faith in its own abilities. The town had developed what can only be described as a siege mentality. This means most people behaved as if an attack could come at any time and from anywhere and were forever looking over their shoulders.

The Custodians of Concord, the elite group of citizens chosen to restore order to the town after Aldor's first attack, also decided to make security a primary focus. They came up with the new motto 'Safety First', which began to crop up in general conversation, not just in science prac classes at Drabville Elementary. The Custodians were also discussing a management plan but had not yet achieved consensus. Should Drabville demonstrate its outrage at what had occurred by investing heavily in surveillance and weaponry? Or should the town adopt a defiantly *business-as-usual* approach? Milli's mother, Rosemary Klompet, was a strong supporter of the latter course. If Drabville compromised on its values, she argued vehemently, it would mean an even bigger victory for Aldor. They should be careful by all means, but not regress into old practices of repression.

And what of our friends, Milli and Ernest? How were they affected by this new wave of conservatism that had washed over their town?

After their performance at the Shreckal Caverns some years ago, when they had rescued the townsfolk's shadows, Milli and Ernest had found themselves hailed as heroes. But their latest encounter with Lord Aldor had not had the same result; in fact, quite the reverse. Given Milli and Ernest's history of getting themselves into hot water, many of the parents considered them responsible for the abduction of their children. Wasn't it interesting, the whispered speculation went, how *that pair* always seemed to be at the centre of any catastrophe. Clearly they were a bad influence and their parents were blatantly remiss in allowing them to roam around so freely looking for trouble.

If you are wondering why these parents placed the blame squarely on Milli's and Ernest's shoulders when they had in fact saved their children's lives, there is a simple explanation. Whenever anything goes seriously wrong, it is human nature to want to point the finger at someone. Somehow this makes people feel better. Once a culprit has been identified, people feel more in control and, better still, not at all responsible themselves. There are many cases in history of individuals being made into scapegoats to carry the responsibility for some catastrophic event. In 1692 in Salem,

Massachusetts for example, the townsfolk could not find explanations for various events such as illness or strange behaviour and therefore concluded that Satan was loose in Salem. They branded certain people as witches and believed that if they executed every accused witch in the village then all strangeness would cease.

It was very simple to accuse somebody back in 1692. Nowadays you need *evidence* to convict a person in court and send them to prison. In Salem, all you needed to do was visit the magistrate and say, 'That girl mutters under her breath' or 'I've seen her chanting in the forest', and it was enough to have a person convicted and hanged at Gallows Hill. If someone fell ill and suffered spasms or convulsions, or talked in their sleep, they were immediately assumed to be under the enchantment of a witch. Anyone known to be on bad terms with the afflicted became a suspect and was put on trial. Often, young girls would pretend to be possessed; they'd go limp, roll back their eyes and writhe and scream on the ground, making peculiar animal noises. When asked to name her tormentor, the girl would go rigid and point her

13

finger at someone in the room. Let me tell you now, if you were that person, you were more or less DONE FOR. There was nothing you could do to defend yourself if someone claimed you were making them intentionally ill through the use of black magic. Of course, you could always drop to the ground, start writhing and screaming yourself, and accuse somebody else of bewitching you.

Luckily, the mothers of Drabville were too enlightened for lynching or stoning people and contented themselves with malicious gossip and sidelong glances to liven up their coffee mornings.

Some people went so far as to suggest that Lord Aldor's hatred of Milli and Ernest was the main reason he persisted in terrorising the town. It was vengeance against *them* that had drawn him back a second time. Even though Drabvillians were far too polite to ever express these ideas openly, there are, as we know, more subtle ways of making people feel excluded. The occasional comment picked up at the dinner table found its way into the schoolyard, and Milli and Ernest noticed they received fewer invitations to birthday parties and the like these days. It made them feel a little unsettled and more than a little bit lonely. They compensated by devoting more time to their studies (harder for Milli than for Ernest) and by relying on each other for entertainment.

CHAPTER TWO

A New Phase Begins

Their adventures in the Conjurors' Realm had had very different effects on Milli and Ernest.

Ernest's entire belief system had been called into question and he found himself thinking about the world and his place in it. He pondered ideas like the purpose of his own life and the concept of contentment. If evil was such a powerful force in the world, what could one do to ensure one's immunity against it? Could one individual really change things for the better? What avenues were available to a child who wanted to improve the world? These were the burning questions that consumed Ernest's free

16

time. One morning the answer presented itself. What the world needed more of, Ernest decided, was not politicians but poets! Poets, as a rule, were not short-term thinkers and therefore could really make a difference. He knew from his classical studies that the ancient poets had done more than construct pretty verse; they were highly regarded and could be instrumental in shaping public opinion. Some, admittedly, had ended their days in exile but the power of their words lived on to shape modern civilisation.

Ernest padded down to breakfast, still in slippers and a dressing gown, to share his epiphany with the people he held most dear.

'I want you to be the first to know that from this day forward I go out into the world as a sonneteer!'

His father barely looked up from his morning paper as he muttered, 'Good for you, son.' His mother seemed more concerned with making sure his siblings ate over their plates so as to minimise the crumbs she would need to sweep up later. His siblings (even though their mouths were full) showed enough interest to ask whether a sonneteer was related to a musketeer and what worldly goods Ernest might part with in order to follow this new direction. All in all, the reaction could hardly be described as enthusiastic.

That same afternoon, at the Drabville Baths (a dome-shaped building made up almost entirely of mosaic tiles in various shades of blue and green) Ernest broke the news to his best friend. The response he received from her was certainly less dispassionate.

'Why do you say something like this *now*?' Milli said, clenching her fists and rolling her eyes dramatically.

'What's wrong with now?' Ernest looked around furtively to check whether there was something else going on that he'd somehow missed.

'The last thing we need right now is for you to go all funny.'

'Well, I don't think any humour will be immediately apparent,' Ernest said, trying to sound appeasing.

'Sonneteers can still play, right?'

'Of course.'

Milli was sufficiently heartened by this to

share an announcement of her own. 'I've decided something too, ' she said, her eyes shining.

'Really?' said Ernest, in a tone that meant: *this should be good.*

'I've decided not to grow up,' Milli told him.

'How interesting. And when did you come to this decision?'

'Just this morning. I'm afraid you shall have to go on without me.'

'I'm sorry to hear that,' said Ernest, trying his best to twist his amusement into a sympathetic smile.

'You think I'm joking!'

'Don't be a twit, Milli — you can't arrest your own growth. It's a biological impossibility.'

'I think I can, if I concentrate really hard.'

'No, you can't. It's nothing to do with concentration. I assume you'll continue your consumption of food and water during this period of non-development?'

'Of course. I don't plan to die of starvation.'

'Then you'll continue to grow,' Ernest said plainly.

'I could give up healthy foods like dairy, lean meat and leafy vegetables,' Milli suggested.

19

'That won't stop you growing; it just means you'll grow with bad skin and poor eyesight. Why would you want to stay a child forever anyway?'

Milli paused a moment before offering a reply. 'Well, what attraction can you see in growing up?'

Ernest, who was sitting with his legs dangling over the pool's edge, pensively rubbed his chin with his hand. 'You have a point there,' he said.

Milli had been making similarly ridiculous pronouncements at home. At first, the other Klompets had raised their eyebrows in amusement but it had now got to the point where her family felt as though they had to walk on eggshells around her.

'Why does our house have to have such ugly windows?' Milli demanded one day.

Sensing trouble, her parents exchanged cautionary glances and tried to defuse the mounting tension.

'Ugly is such a relative term,' said Mr Klompet, trying to sound light-hearted.

'How does potato pizza for dinner sound?'

20

asked Milli's mother, trying to change the subject.

But Milli wouldn't be sidetracked.

'I need my room to have casement windows. It's not fair that it doesn't. Can't they be changed?'

'Not without incurring considerable expense,' said Rosie, quickly running out of patience.

'Why, Capricious Daughter, this urgent need for casement windows?' Milli's father was foolish enough to ask.

'Isn't it obvious? I need windows that open outwards so Peter Pan can visit. He's probably been trying for months but he can't squeeze in!'

(For any of you unfamiliar with the story of *Peter Pan*, it is about a boy who lives in a magical place called Neverland where you never grow up. He visits a girl called Wendy Darling by climbing through her nursery window.)

'Well then, I promise to give the installation of casement windows some quite serious consideration,' Mr Klompet said.

Milli's fractious mood continued. 'Don't you think this family needs a holiday after everything that's happened?' she said.

'Now that isn't such a bad idea,' Rosie replied, 'if Dorkus could be talked round. Where should we go, do you think?'

'Wherever the Fountain of Youth is most likely to be located, of course. Somewhere in Europe, I imagine, but we need to find out and go straightaway. There isn't a minute to lose.'

By now you may be raising your own eyebrows in disapproval and thinking, BRING BACK CORPORAL PUNISHMENT!, but Milli was not being difficult for the sake of it. In fact, in her own mind she could not see that she was being anything but reasonable. As often happens with children who are left to their own devices and end up relying mainly on the workings of their imagination for company, Milli continued to believe unequivocally that anything was possible.

Both the Klompets and the Perriclofs concluded that their children's odd behaviour was the result of trauma and their current lack of popularity, and tried to be understanding. Milli and Ernest were encouraged to take Stench for long walks or given small errands to run to keep them from brooding.

It was on one of these walks with Stench that they found something interesting happening right under their noses. Change was something towards which Drabville had recently developed a reactionary attitude, but Milli and Ernest wandered into one part of town where change seemed to be taking place relatively unobstructed. This change had to do with construction, and although Milli and Ernest were the first to stumble upon it, any family taking a Sunday morning stroll through Poxxley Gardens could not have missed it. The old ruin, Hog House, which had once served as the town mayor's private residence, appeared to be undergoing extensive renovation.

Hog House was, of course, the site of the children's incarceration by the mad Mr and Mrs Mayor. Their adventures there now seemed so long ago. They both shuddered at the memory of what had gone on behind those doors.

But despite their unease, Milli and Ernest had not outgrown the lure of detective work and were intrigued. They observed the work in silence for some time before deciding there was something not quite right about it.

'How strange that someone should want to rebuild on this site,' Milli said. 'No one's been near it since we left and some people even say it's haunted.'

'Haunted or not, it was bound to happen,' Ernest said, trying to sound practical. 'The real question is, what are they building?'

Stench, excited by the possibility of new smells, strained on his leash, but when they got closer the children saw that wire fencing had been erected around the building site, both as a safety precaution and to keep inquisitive intruders out.

The mystery surrounding the new building was fuelled in subsequent days by the mumbled answers children received whenever they quizzed their parents about what was happening at the big old place behind the park. Their parents wouldn't give an immediate reply; and when they did it was far from satisfactory, with responses along the lines of *community centre* or *residential development*. There were serious inconsistencies in the range of explanations given. But as building sites are generally not

24

that exciting to children unless they are permitted to fossick amongst the rubble, the matter was gradually dropped and the construction carried on in the background, given no more than a cursory glance by those who happened to be walking by.

Milli and Ernest, of course, did not lose interest. Hog House remained, in their minds a place of mystery and adventure. They tried on several occasions to get a closer look but were prevented by barricades and workmen in yellow safety helmets jumping out at them. They had to confine their investigation to keeping a close eye on the flurry of activity — scaffolding being erected, barricades shifted to allow access to bobcats and trucks, workmen pushing wheelbarrows filled with all manner of building materials. But if they lingered too long they were promptly told to 'Skedaddle'. Although the building itself was too far away for them to make out any detail, one thing they did notice each time they were drawn to the site was the rapidity of progress. As for the workers, they didn't recognise a single face amongst them. Obviously they had all been brought in from other villages specially for the project. That, too, was very interesting.

One afternoon, when the children's interest was finally starting to wane, Stench broke free of their hold and crashed through an opening in the fence, eager to chase down something that had caught his eye. Fortunately, the workmen were at a safe distance packing up for the day, so the children were able to scramble through after Stench. When they finally retrieved the panting dog, they found the object that had drawn his attention was a silver bell, no bigger than a thumbnail, glittering in the afternoon sun. It was an incongruous object to find amidst building rubble and plaster dust. Milli bent to retrieve it, but the bell slipped continually from her fingers and could not be grasped. They made a hasty retreat when Stench began to bark in mounting frustration.

'What do you make of that?' Milli asked.

Ernest shook his head. 'Must be a relic from Hog House.'

'Wherever it's from, that's no ordinary bell,' said Milli. 'Should we report it?'

Ernest rolled his eyes at her. 'And risk mass

hysteria, not to mention losing the freedom we've only just started to enjoy? I don't think so.'

When Milli and Ernest and the children of Drabville returned from the Conjurors' Realm, they did not return alone. With them came two freckled twins with limbs the width of matchsticks and a weather-beaten old woman wearing a hairnet and lugging a suitcase stuffed full of cooking utensils. The arrival of Finn and Fennel and Nonna Luna in Drabville generated considerable interest amongst the townsfolk. Who were these elastic acrobatic twins who wore far-away expressions and insisted on sewing sequins on their school uniforms so as to feel more at home? Who was this old woman as gnarled as an ancient tree whose dishes could persuade even the most lethargic of men to mow the lawn? Could these visitors be trusted if they came from a world once overseen by Lord Aldor? But it did not take long for the good nature of the new arrivals to become obvious and all suspicion vanished. After all, how could Drabville not welcome with open arms individuals who had been so pivotal in their children's escape?

Finn and Fennel's assimilation into Drabville wasn't without some early mishaps. Due to their upbringing the twins were a little short on social graces. They tended to laugh too loudly and point at anything that delighted them. At first, they walked around Drabville in a state of wonder, especially struck each time a citizen performed an act of courtesy or kindness. They were amazed to see the fit willingly give up their seats on buses for the elderly or infirm or to hear one person begging the pardon of another they had accidentally knocked against. They would duck instinctively if someone tried to shake their hand, and anything free — like sugar cubes on café tables — was a source of great excitement. It took some time before they could be dissuaded from pocketing sugar cubes when they thought the staff weren't looking. The townsfolk, however, were patient, understanding that these children had grown up accustomed to cruelty and indifference.

Initially the twins had stayed with the Klompets but then a lady with impeccable credentials offered to adopt them. She was none other than teacher and librarian Miss Linear, who was positively ecstatic about the prospect of offering the twins a home. Miss Linear had never got around to having children of her own. This was ascribed to the well-known fact that she had not as yet found a member of the opposite sex whose company she could tolerate long enough to share a cup of tea with let alone contemplate the idea of breeding with. Milli suspected Miss Linear's lack of a partner might have something to do with the revolting mustard-coloured cardigan she wore every day of the year, coupled with woollen stockings and brown brogues as unflattering as bricks. But Miss Linear made no such connection, proclaiming that she had yet to meet a man whose company she preferred to that of her cat, Pocket.

After only a month of living with Miss Linear, Finn and Fennel had filled out, and their eyes had lost their haunted look and gained a new lustre. The twins wore with pride the matching vests Miss Linear knitted them, and pounced on the printed word like hungry

29

wolves. They started by reading bus tickets and the jokes on the backs of cereal boxes, but quickly progressed to books and became voracious and critical readers. It was Finn's personal mission to read every title in the town library's historical fiction collection, whilst Fennel loved nothing more than a good romance in which the hero rode a black stallion and the heroine always wore white. Neither, however, could bear to read books in the fantasy genre.

Nonna Luna was a hit from the start. By selling some Lampo family heirlooms originally intended for her grandson, she was able to set up a nice little business she called The Pasta Train. Before long she had a massive following amongst the mothers of Drabville. Not only did her food develop a reputation for quality and generous portions, but Nonna made her pasta in full view of her customers. It wasn't a bad way to spend your lunch break, standing outside Nonna's front window, watching her skilled hands knead and work the dough, then cut it into various shapes and sizes before hanging it up to dry. Spectators often broke into spontaneous applause and invariably bought something for dinner. Sauces, too, were available in little tubs and needed only gentle heating once you got home. Some type of dish from The Pasta Train appeared on Drabville dinner tables at least once a week after Nonna's arrival, and suddenly mothers found they had more time for important matters like visits to the hairdresser or those golf lessons they'd been forever putting off.

The other thing Nonna introduced to Drabville was real coffee. Up until then Drabville coffee had been a bitter brew, made by pouring hot water over brown granules that bore a remarkable resemblance to rat poison. But now the townsfolk could choose between a velvety smooth *cappuccino* or an *espresso* guaranteed to recharge one's batteries just in time for that morning board meeting. In the more cosmopolitan Drabville it wasn't long before people started saying 'Ciao' instead of their usual 'Cheerio for now'.

Nonna Luna refused to dwell on past experiences; she had drawn a curtain across them. If Milli or Ernest ever attempted to engage her in conversation about their time at Battalion

Minor, or Queen Fidelis and her Kingdom of Mirth, she would immediately put up a hand in warning and offer them a pastry to change the subject. Finn and Fennel were so grateful to finally be part of a caring home that they too had little interest in recalling the past. But Milli and Ernest had no intention of forgetting and often privately shared their recollections. They could not look at a patch of wild mushrooms growing in the woods, or a cluster of daisies by the roadside, without being transported back to Mirth and reliving the magic they had experienced there. In fact, for Milli and Ernest there wasn't much that did not trigger memories of the Conjurors' Realm.

The normally reserved Ernest made a huge admission to Milli one afternoon. 'Sometimes I actually miss the Realm,' he said with a degree of surprise.

'Me too,' agreed Milli, not the least bit surprised. 'Things have changed too much around here,' she complained. 'Nobody seems to have fun any more.'

'Perhaps it's time we stopped thinking about fun,' Ernest suggested without much conviction.

'After all, we start senior school next week and there'll be plenty of study to keep us occupied.'

'Thanks, Ernest, for those words of comfort.'

'What I mean is, the concept of fun can be redefined as you get older. It doesn't mean you stop having it.'

Milli gave him a ferocious frown. 'Anything that has to be *redefined* doesn't sound much like fun to me.'

We can hardly blame Milli for feeling this way. Who could welcome a return to routine after visiting a world filled with such wonders as convicts imprisoned in cobblestones, giants, hags, shiny citadels made of precious stones, and shopkeeper pixies that like to play practical jokes on their customers? I am not saying that Milli did not relish the security of home; merely that being home and safe did not necessarily obliterate the thrills of their past experiences. Even Ernest gave himself away once by unthinkingly asking whether Admiral's Beard was on the menu at the local pub, and on more than one occasion Milli found herself asking her mother if she might have three soots instead of pennies to spend at the corner store.

CHAPTER THREE

Birds
of a Feather

oon there really wasn't the time to reminisce about the past, or speculate about Hog House or slippery silver bells. When Mrs Klompet had discovered that the children were snooping around the building site, she emphatically forbade them to visit again. Not wanting to cause further trouble Milli and Ernest listened. Besides there were other things for them to worry about.

Milli and Ernest started as juniors at St Erudite's Academy and their new school presented them with such a host of requirements and expectations that survival soon became their prime objective. No sooner did they feel that they had things under control than another challenge was thrown at them. Never in their entire lives had they had to manage their time so carefully, but now it was a necessity if they were to complete what was required of them and not fall behind. Suddenly every half-hour had to be accounted for, and leisure became something you had to block out time for along with everything else. Needless to say, Ernest fared better than Milli in this regard.

St Erudite's Academy was no ordinary school; it was the oldest and most well-regarded secondary school in the region. It had been carefully selected by Milli's and Ernest's parents as it offered a wide range of academic studies and was the only school that still taught Latin. It had an unrivalled music department with numerous orchestras and ensembles, as well as lush sports ovals, tennis courts and a newly built pool and gymnasium, and a veritable smorgasbord of co-curricular activities. In addition it boasted an impressive array of luminaries amongst its alumni. Ernest had been granted a full scholarship and was very conscious of living up to the expectations associated with this position. He regularly reminded Milli that she should feel privileged to have been accepted to St Erudite's, as many were on waiting lists and had been since birth. Milli rolled her eyes but didn't argue the point.

St Erudite's school motto was 'Plan, Strive, Soar'. In keeping with this theme, someone had come up with the ingenious if corny idea of identifying the different levels by bird species. First years were Sparrows, second years Starlings, the middle years were Kestrels and Hawks, and by the time you reached your final years of secondary education you were first an Eagle and finally an Owl. How eagles could precede owls wasn't immediately clear to Milli and Ernest, but after some heated debate they decided it probably had something to do with the value of wisdom over skill and confidence.

One chilly Monday morning a few weeks into term, the children shuffled their way to school carrying bulging satchels, violin cases (both had just started lessons) and their art folios. They had missed the school bus, as a result of Milli being unable to find her shoe, and were now forced to walk despite the foul weather. Drabville's usual school calendar had been revised to accommodate the kidnapped children's return, so it was already late October by the time lessons resumed. The day was overcast and the wind seemed to bite right through them. There was snow on the distant hills; their tips appeared only as a whitish blur. The children hoped the streets, too, would soon disappear under a layer of white.

Milli couldn't suppress a smile as she glanced at Ernest. Mrs Perriclof had bundled him up as if his destination were the Antarctic rather than St Erudite's. The black coat he was wearing over his school blazer was made from a quilted fabric that made him look as though he was encased in bubble wrap. His arms stuck out a little from his sides and his usual walk was restricted to a waddle. From a distance he looked like an overgrown penguin. He also wore thick mittens, a knitted scarf wrapped tightly around his neck and a hat lined with sheep's wool pulled firmly over his head. All Milli could see of him was the tip of his very pink nose. This was one morning when Ernest was envious of his siblings who, considered too unprepared for the demands of 'institutionalised education', remained at home under the tutelage of their mother, an enterprise so exhausting that Mrs Perriclof often had to have a lie-down in the afternoons.

'It really is too cold to be outside,' Milli said, turning up the collar of her school blazer and sniffing audibly as they made their way down the street. She had been battling a minor cold for weeks now but unfortunately it hadn't developed into anything more serious, like bronchitis or pneumonia. It was really of no use whatsoever — bad enough to block her nose so she couldn't sleep properly, but not bad enough to warrant any time off school.

'*Thou knowest, winter tames man, woman and beast,*' Ernest said as Milli blew her nose noisily into a hanky. He had to tilt his head right back to look at her, so low was his hat pulled over his eyes.

'*What?*' Milli said, but regretted it almost immediately.

'I am quoting from the Bard. It's remarkable how poetry can provide us with insights into everyday life.'

Even though Milli knew Ernest ought not to be encouraged, her curiosity was piqued. 'Quoting from a bird?' she repeated. Her ears were also slightly blocked.

'Not bird, *Bard*. It's another name for the most famous of all playwrights — even you must have heard of Shakespeare.'

'Course I have,' Milli said defensively. 'I just got confused when you called him a bird.'

'I plan to be an aficionado by the time the year's out.'

Milli was finding Ernest's train of thought increasingly difficult to follow. 'A fishy what?'

'Very funny. It's Spanish and means to become really passionate about something. Have you seen the posters advertising the competition the library's running — *Who Said What?* They give you dozens of quotes from Shakespeare and you have to name the character who said it.'

'Didn't he write a lot of plays?'

'Twenty-three in total, but I'm hoping they'll focus on the better-known ones.'

'What's the prize?' Milli asked, more interested in suppressing the sneeze that was coming than in Ernest's answer.

'A leather-bound edition of his complete works for the school library.'

'Wow. And for the winner?'

'Only glory,' Ernest replied, clicking his tongue. 'Sweet, sweet glory.'

When they reached the turn-off for Drabville Elementary, Milli unconsciously made towards it and Ernest had to pluck her back and steer her left. Milli made this mistake every time they were forced to walk, particularly when she was preoccupied.

Within weeks of arriving at their new school both Milli and Ernest felt far removed from their old lives. So much more was expected of them. Classes were held in various musty buildings sometimes at opposite ends of the grounds and the children often had to rush in order to avoid a Late Mark. There were books and folders, diaries and sports bags not to mention special equipment for electives to juggle as they made their way through corridors crowded with seniors who chatted away in doorways and never seemed to be in a hurry.

We know that organisation was not one of Milli's strong points, so if it hadn't been for

Ernest she would have been a total disaster. 'Don't forget your safety glasses — it's Science after Oratory,' he would remind her as they both tried to wrangle their things out of tiny wooden lockers on the bottom row.

Milli continued to miss her old school longer than any of her peers. She missed the intimacy of it and the leisurely pace, how a whole day could stretch out in front of you, full of promise. She missed the afternoons of reading in the corner set aside expressly for that purpose and scattered with an array of colourful floor cushions you could arrange for your own comfort. She missed the projects that could consume hours of your time on presentation alone before you felt they were impressive enough to submit for assessment. Their classroom at Drabville Elementary had been a welcoming place with every available surface displaying their dioramas of the solar system and models of the pyramids. Milli envied Finn and Fennel, who were still there, having been held back a year to allow them to catch up on all the things they'd missed during their years with the Lampo Circus. Milli was finding the transition to senior school difficult, and although she was growing accustomed to St Erudite's culture, she really had to wonder about the pedagogy (a word she had recently learned from Ernest) behind some of its practices. How could poorly heated, Spartan classrooms be conducive to learning? And how ludicrous was it that access to students' lockers was barred other than at break times, which meant you had to remember to collect what you needed for several lessons in a row. And that meant you had to remember what those lessons were. Often there wasn't the time to be searching for timetables (sensible Ernest had taped a copy of his to the inside of his locker door). Milli was forever picking up the wrong folder or leaving behind her Mathemat. For the life of her she couldn't see why most of their classes couldn't be held in the one room, where they could have assigned desks to store their things in. And how hard could it be to fit pegs to the walls to hang up the blazers that barely fitted inside their minuscule lockers?

Apart from the physical challenges of life at St Erudite's the students seemed a far less cohesive group. There were the twelve prefects with shiny badges pinned to their lapels, teachers who strode through the halls with their academic gowns fluttering behind them, and students grouped into factions based on skill or sophistication. Milli was fascinated by the seniors; the boys with their easy humour and shirts only half tucked and the girls with their manicured nails and glossy smiles. Once a boy called James Woods (Woodsy to his friends) who was the debating captain had given Milli a cheeky wink after catching her staring. She had flushed deeply and had become so disoriented she had to be led away by a baffled Ernest.

But the sudden decline in status was perhaps the most difficult change to come to terms with. Both Milli and Ernest had achieved what can only be described as a *profile* at Drabville Elementary. They were always the ones who took the lead, whether in debating, chess or school theatrical productions. At St Erudite's the competition was tougher; they had to prove their worth all over again. Milli tried out for a couple of sporting teams but found she lacked the required speed and agility. Ernest auditioned for the end-of-year production of *Macbeth* and was seriously miffed when he was cast as Banquo's son, Fleance, a character who spoke two lines in the entire play. Ernest wasn't used to being upstaged by older boys with booming voices and greater 'stage presence'. As for debating, both children had been placed in a beginners' team full of stuttering students so nervous they kept getting their palm cards out of order.

St Erudite's Academy was also very focused on the upholding of tradition. Teachers were always impressing upon students the importance of adhering to the rules. 'Without rules,' one ancient master was fond of repeating, 'there would be anarchy, and you know what would happen then, don't you? Civilisation as we know it would crumble.' He always doubled over when he said this, as if he himself were on the verge of crumbling. Wearing the correct uniform was also reinforced constantly, especially when public appearances were required. Milli had improved significantly in this department, with some assistance from her mother, but it still struck her as a dreadful waste of time. The boys' uniform comprised grey wool shorts, a sky blue vest and gold striped tie. The girls wore a pleated navy skirt and pale blue blouse with a round collar. In summer, both boys and girls were required to wear a straw boater displaying the school crest on their way to and from school. Milli's boater was already looking rather battered from having been mistaken by Stench as part of his bedding, and she hadn't even worn it yet. Both sexes also wore the mandatory grey blazer and black lace-up shoes. For someone as free-spirited as Milli, St Erudite's felt like an institution. If it hadn't been for the kindness of one teacher, the whole experience would have been even more alienating.

Even the most conservative of schools often make allowances for those involved in the performing or creative arts. It is generally thought that these individuals occupy more rarefied fields and thus must be permitted greater freedoms. Milli's and Ernest's home-room teacher, Miss Mildew Macaw, fell into this category. The most obvious thing that set her apart from the rest of the staff was her dress code. She wore silk scarves, sometimes in the place of a belt or wound around her head like a turban, oriental skirts that almost trailed the floor and jingled when she moved, tights with jungle patterns, and flat silver ballet shoes decorated with bows or sequins. She also had a rather extensive collection of embroidered vests. Mildew Macaw liked to wear handcrafted jewellery (mostly made by artist friends) such as polished wooden beads as large as chestnuts or brooches in the shape of tropical flowers. Sometimes she wore clothes pegs painted in assorted colours in her hair. Often, when she needed her hands to be free, she stored her paintbrushes in the coil of her silver bun. In short, she was a character; although less enlightened students preferred other terms, like 'Mad Macaw' to describe her.

Milli and Ernest loved her. Miss Macaw was thin, of medium height but long-limbed, with bony hands that she waved about whenever something excited her, which was often. She loved to share little confidences with her 'special group'. On the very first day she had told them about her past life as an accomplished potter, the collapse of her disastrous marriage to a German baron who had absconded with her inheritance leaving her virtually destitute, the digestive problems of Buster her bull terrier, and her determination to eat only home-grown vegetables. She also informed them that these days her artistic endeavours were confined to school holidays as the more important business of teaching took up the bulk of her time and energy.

Aside from being their form mistress, Miss M, as she was eventually dubbed, took them for Ceramics as well as a subject called Conflict and Catastrophes, which covered a mishmash of topics from the Battle of Hastings to tornadoes and other natural disasters. Ceramics was by far Milli's favourite class, even though Miss Macaw insisted on playing Gregorian chants in the background for *inspiration*. Even Ernest didn't seem to object to donning his smock and sinking his fingers into a clump of moist clay. In Ceramics they learned to *sledge* and *slurry* as they made masks, chimes and coil pots. Miss Macaw was a veritable mine of information when it came to art history. Various pieces of information would be dropped like pebbles into whatever discussion they might be having at the time.

'The ancient Greeks were fine ceramic artists,' she rhapsodised one afternoon as she strolled around the art-room, stopping to give artistic advice as she went. 'We use much the same techniques today some two thousand years later. Now, isn't that amazing?' Miss Macaw stopped by Milli's table and bent over to show her how to smooth out the lumps in the food bowl she was making for Stench. As Milli listened to her explanation, she happened to look out of the classroom windows at a rapidly greying sky. Just for a moment she indulged in her old pastime of trying to discern faces in the clouds. There was definitely the head of a horse, she decided, followed by what looked like a bowl of porridge. After a while she thought she could make out an ancient face with a hooked nose that seemed to be looking straight back at her. There was something about that face ... something horribly familiar that made her breath catch in her throat. Stench's bowl almost slipped from her grasp and she looked around for Ernest to calm her fears but he was unloading the kiln in a far corner. When Milli looked out the window again, the clouds had shifted position and the face was gone.

When St Erudite's came into view, Milli and Ernest were alarmed to see the entrance area deserted, apart from a few gardeners unloading wheelbarrows and beginning work on the garden beds. They bolted through the gates, down the gravel path and up the flight of external stairs that took them to Sparrow House, a maroon-brick rectangular wing in the oldest part of the school.

In her haste to keep up with Ernest, who was determined to avoid a Late Mark, Milli lost her footing on the stairs, dropped her folio and watched its contents (three-dimensional drawings of streetscapes) float down to ground level.

Fortunately, discipline was an aspect of education that interested Miss Macaw the least and she merely smiled indulgently at the children when they finally made an appearance and waved them to their seats.

While Miss Macaw marked the roll, the Bulletin Monitor, Nigel Molting, read aloud the class announcements. Nigel thought himself very important, and liked to emulate teachers by stopping, raising his eyebrows and waiting for silence every time someone so much as whispered; a habit that had earned him the nickname of Sir. Sir was just reminding anyone who was interested that tomorrow was the last day for returning money and permission slips for the Literary Breakfast when an unexpected crackle came from the loudspeaker. Classes were only ever interrupted by a loudspeaker announcement in the event of an emergency. All heads turned towards the speaker. Even Miss Macaw screwed up her face and gave it her full attention.

'All Sparrows and Starlings are to report to the main hall for an assembly immediately after roll call.' As the speaker crackled into silence again, a buzz of speculation spread through the classroom.

CHAPTER FOUR

News at Assembly

t Erudite's main hall was vast and formidable. It was long and airy with vaulted ceilings and heavy wood panelling. In the foyer hung portraits of previous headmasters and benefactors, and there were rows of glass cabinets housing sporting and academic trophies, as well as photographs of the school's most recent theatrical extravaganza. By the time the Sparrows filed into the main hall, most of the junior school teachers were perched on a platform at the front like a row of bats in their academic gowns. Their eyes darted around the hall like radar beams, scanning for students whose appearance or behaviour might be considered less than exemplary.

Gloria Humpenstar and Edweed Gosling, the head girl and head boy, approached the lectern. 'Please stand for the official party,' they said in unison.

The students rose en masse as the official party appeared as if from nowhere and proceeded slowly down the centre aisle. It was headed by Dr Publius Hurtle, Headmaster of the Academy, a short, well-fed man with a balding pate and steel grey eyes who wore a purple sash on his gown that denoted his academic standing. He was followed by others with varying degrees of responsibility. Milli observed that so weighty were their gowns that it seemed to result in some very bad posture. Miss Simper, Head of Sparrow House, was particularly slanted.

When the party reached the podium and were finally seated, the heads of school spoke again. 'Please remain standing for the school song.'

The notes of an organ rose and crashed through the hall and the official party led the singing. Milli joined in, her voice faltering a little. She was still unsure of the verses and had to keep stealing sidelong glances at Ernest who, naturally, had memorised them all by the second day of school.

St Erudite, our hearts will always cherish you
The big draughty school upon the hill!
To you we owe our standards.
Obstacles we never will fear.

Through your hallowed halls and stony arches
We walk with dignity and pride.
Our hearts swell up with feeling
To know your spirit is always by our side!

With our motto emblazoned on our pockets
We face challenges with serenity!
St Erudite, may your teachings guide us
In our search for identity!

Well versed in all the classics
But modern thinkers through and through,
Whatever path our lives may take us
Know that our hearts reside with you!

Oh leap for joy! Shout to the skies!
St Erudite, St Erudite!
Wherever life may take us
May we be forever true!

When the song was finished and everyone seated again, Dr Hurtle rose to address them. He cleared his throat, pushed up his spectacles and then broke into an uncharacteristic grin. In fact, the usually sober-faced headmaster was beaming from ear to ear.

'Good morning, Sparrows and Starlings, and welcome to another week at St Erudite's. I'm sure you must all be wondering what could be so important as to justify the interruption of your lessons this morning. You will note that this assembly involves only the juniors as what I have to say pertains especially to you. I have no doubt that my announcement will result in much excitement and I now ask that you curb that excitement once you resume class so the rest of the day may proceed as normal.'

How ridiculous, thought Milli, to be asked to curb your excitement before you even knew what it was you were meant to be excited about. She noticed that the headmaster was carrying a rolled newspaper under one arm.

'I don't suppose any of you have had an opportunity to see this morning's paper?' he asked. Dr Hurtle's questions were usually of a rhetorical nature and so his pause for a reply was met only with an uncertain silence. 'I thought not, but let me tell you that it contains an item which I am sure will be of great interest to you. Rather than describing its contents, allow me to read it to you in its entirety.'

He unrolled what looked to be a copy of the Drabville *Bugle* and read aloud the following front-page article:

TINY TOWN, VALIANT HEARTS!

To commemorate the recent bravery and resilience shown by the children of Drabville, billionaire philanthropist and renowned toymaker Gustav Von Gobstopper has most generously funded the construction of a Toy Arcade right here in our town.

The construction of the arcade, situated on the site formerly known as Hog House, is due for completion within days and has been kept secret from all children in order not to spoil the surprise.

The reclusive Von Gobstopper was living quietly in his Austrian castle when news of our intrepid adventurers reached him. So touched by the story was he that he felt compelled to do something in response. Some months ago Von Gobstopper's representatives approached Drabville authorities with an idea they were delighted to support.

The arcade will officially open this coming Friday, and the juniors of St Erudite's Academy have been invited to make the inaugural visit. As the arcade's first visitors the children will have their photos taken and be invited to sign the official guest book. The students will be taken on a tour of the facility and will enjoy a complimentary afternoon tea in the Teddy Bear Bakery. This special group of children will also have access to items from Von Gobstopper's private toy collection never before seen by members of the general public. Members of the media will not be permitted to intrude on this special experience and have been asked to show restraint.

The world has been stunned by Von Gobstopper's sudden emergence from retirement. Von Gobstopper is widely hailed as a master toymaker and a genius and Drabville can only feel privileged to have been chosen to

56

showcase his talents. This event may well change the course of history for the little out-of-the-way town and put Drabville on the map. Some have predicted that the arcade will prove a popular tourist destination, drawing visitors from around the globe.

Mr Von Gobstopper himself was unavailable for comment, but one of his staff conveyed on his behalf his wish 'to pay homage to some inspirational children'. A spokesperson for the Custodians of Concord, Rosemary Klompet, said she could not be happier. 'We all feel that the children deserve this recognition, given what they have been through. We are very fortunate that Mr Von Gobstopper shares our view. He has devoted his life to delighting the young through his unique toys and I can think of no worthier recipients of his generosity than the children of this town.'

Hildebeast Wordypants

Dr Hurtle's admonition that things should proceed as normal was a touch unrealistic. The children could not focus on anything other than what they had just been told. They made their way back to their classrooms while the older students they passed gave them covetous looks and grumbled about injustice. Classrooms were full of excited whispers even the sternest of teachers could not suppress. In the end many just gave up and modified their lesson plans accordingly so that in English they postponed Subject and Predicate and wrote Haikus about their favourite toys.

You may well be wondering what all the commotion was about. Toys are simply toys to many of us, and we're not too bothered which company makes them. As long as they open, shut, squeak, roar, fly across the room or perform whatever other function they are designed to perform, we are happy. But a toy made by Gustav Von Gobstopper was no regular toy. It was unique. Von Gobstopper toys didn't come off an assembly line; each one was individually handcrafted with an astounding attention to detail. It is said that one of Michelangelo's admirers, standing before one of the master's sculptures, was so overwhelmed by its lifelike quality that he invoked it to speak. Such was the awe you felt if you were lucky enough to own a

Von Gobstopper toy. The man was an artist, and some said his talents were wasted on creating toys for the entertainment of children. But children were bewitched by them and toys with the *Made by Von Gob* seal were coveted and yearned for. Most of Drabville's children had at least one such item in their collection and rarely was it passed on to younger siblings. The Von Gobstopper logo was a red toy box crammed with bears, dolls, trains and trucks, all trying to clamber out to play. On the box in a black script was the message: *Handle with love. Herein lies a friend for life.* And no matter how many knocks or falls the toys suffered, they never dented or broke. Von Gobstopper was to toys what Luis Vuitton is to luggage or Mr Lindt to chocolate. In other words, pretty darn hard to beat.

Although Milli and Ernest had been a little disappointed when their investigations of the activity at Hog House had been brought to an abrupt end, it now all made sense. And it was impossible to resist the contagious excitement that was spreading amongst the first and second years. Not only had Von Gobstopper travelled across continents in recognition of their achievement but he had invested many thousands of dollars to celebrate their return.

'And to think we were suspicious!' Milli commented to Ernest. 'When all along they were planning a surprise!'

'What about the silver bell?' Ernest asked, reluctant to get excited too quickly.

'It's a toy arcade!' Milli scoffed. 'There's bound to be gadgets lying around.' Ernest, who could not dispute this logic, was forced to agree. 'Von Gobstopper must be very generous,' Milli continued. 'I wonder if we'll get to met him?'

'I shouldn't think so. He hasn't been seen in public for the last ten years.'

Ernest's nonchalance irritated Milli who was not done with her dissection and analysis of the news.

Back in class, Ernest made them sit at the desk right at the front of the classroom at a right angle to the teacher's desk. He said he needed to sit there as he had trouble seeing the blackboard but Milli knew it was to ensure he didn't miss something important that might crop up on an end-of-term exam.

* * *

The classroom was poorly ventilated and the arched windows so ancient they only opened a fraction. As a result the room was freezing in winter and permanently stuffy in summer. On shelves on one side resided a dusty globe, a collection of well-worn encyclopaedias and assorted periodicals. A large blackboard took up almost the entire front wall. Sitting on its ledge was a metal tin full of chalk in every colour other than white. Miss Macaw perversely refused to use white, claiming it bleached the colour out of learning. But some colleagues suspected it might have more to do with the Baron's penchant for wearing only suits made of white linen.

When the students arrived for Miss Macaw's lesson they found her smacking the radiator with a ruler in an attempt to fire it up. The radiator was so ineffective that it only reached a cosy temperature towards the end of the day, by which time they were all getting ready to go home.

'Well, well, what astonishing news!' Miss Macaw exclaimed in her sing-song voice. 'And what wonderful timing — so close to Christmas!

You are fortunate children indeed, and I'm sure the experience will be an unforgettable one. But now, in keeping with Dr Hurtle's instruction to maintain a business-as-usual approach, I'd like us to begin looking at the Viking invasions.'

In the time it took Miss Macaw to draw breath, Ernest had the relevant exercise book open and was already entering the date and topic heading. All of Ernest's books were covered in white contact and his personal details were clearly printed on the inside cover. These included his name, telephone number, postal address, date of birth and, in the event of an emergency, his blood type.

Milli asked to borrow some paper.

'No,' Ernest grumbled. 'I don't want my book looking tattered just to bail you out.'

'Take the pages from the middle and it won't make any difference.'

As Ernest was about to reluctantly comply, Milli had one of her brainwaves.

She wasn't going to need his precious paper. Viking invasions was about to be abandoned. She raised her hand to ask the question everyone was itching for.

'Miss Macaw, could you please tell us a little bit about Mr Von Gobstopper?'

Miss Macaw, who loved nothing more than to impart knowledge, needed no further inducement.

'Well,' she began, 'every couple of centuries, the world offers us an individual so remarkable that his contribution changes the course of human history. Gustav Von Gobstopper is one of those people.'

'But he just makes toys, doesn't he?' asked one cynical junior.

Miss Macaw gave an audible gasp, clutched her chest with both hands as if struggling for air, and looked at the child as if she'd just discovered he had a terminal illness.

'You must never, ever, think that!' she implored. 'Von Gobstopper is a legend in his own time, a true artist.'

'Why is he no longer seen or heard of?' Harietta Hapless called out eagerly.

'Sometimes, for artists, the world is just too imperfect to handle,' Miss Macaw explained. 'But Mr Von Gobstopper was not always a famous personage. In fact, he came from rather humble beginnings. Shall we put the Vikings aside for today so you can hear his story? After all, a little background information can only enhance the excursion. Harietta, dear, just shut the door so we don't disturb any of the other classes.'

Being of the opinion that the truth should never be allowed to interfere with a good story, Miss Macaw told them everything she had gleaned from her own reading plus some extras thrown in for effect.

'Gustav Von Gobstopper was born in Austria and grew up there with five brothers and sisters. His family were honest but impoverished and his parents couldn't afford to buy their children expensive toys and games at Christmas or on birthdays. They were so poor, in fact, that a new pair of shoes or socks meant a great deal to them. Every year, Gustav, the youngest of the children, would stand outside the toy store in the town's main street and watch the children of affluent families come out clutching brightly wrapped parcels full of new delights to entertain them when they got home. Gustav would look at the dolls and bears in the toy shop window and imagine conversations with them. He would fantasise about playing with the handcrafted marionettes with their painted faces or about riding on the wooden rocking horse with its gleaming saddle and silky mane. Every year he hoped for even the smallest pocket-sized toy that he could call his own, but no one ever bought it for him.

'His passion for toys did not desert him even as he grew into a young man. Finally, when he was about eighteen, Gustav could stand it no longer. He began to stitch his own toys, scavenging materials and scraps from wherever he could. He discovered that all he needed was a lump of rough wood and a handful of screws to make a toy soldier that walked and talked. He used to take his toys into town in a sack and give them away to those children too poor to ever have toys of their own. One day, when he was squatting on the pavement and showing a little girl how to wind up her clockwork doll, a rich merchant noticed him. It was the man who owned the toy store on the main street. He could see at once that Gustav had a gift and immediately took him on as his apprentice.

When the merchant died, Gustav inherited his shop and business went through the roof. In no time at all his toys became world-renowned and he opened more shops all around the globe.

'As his fame spread, Mr Von Gobstopper could no longer work in his shop as people queued up just to catch a glimpse of him, tried to talk to him and invariably interrupted his concentration. He began to travel widely, looking for characters upon whom he could model his creations. On one of those trips he met his soul mate, the Parisian dancer Pascal Le Plastierre. They married, but Pascal contracted a fever, lapsed into a coma and died, exactly a year to the day of their wedding. Gustav never recovered from his tragic loss and became a recluse. Few have laid eyes on him since. That is why his interest in our little town is all the more astonishing.'

Miss Macaw paused for breath. A glance at the clock told her there was only a minute to the end of the lesson but the faces around her seemed in no hurry to move.

'I can only conclude that your story of abduction and your clever escape touched

Mr Von Gobstopper's philanthropic soul,' she finished. 'And now, thanks to him, we have a toy arcade, the first of its kind, right here in Drabville. And you children will be the first to visit it. What do you say to that!'

Part II

Rewards and Surprises

CHAPTER FIVE

Excursion Fever

School excursions can be a bother for teachers but for students they represent a welcome departure from routine — a light at the end of a dark tunnel, an oasis that offers refuge from the parched desert of classrooms and textbooks. It was little wonder that all of Milli's lethargy had evaporated by the time she skipped her way down Peppercorn Place at the end of the day. A toy arcade erected in their honour and constructed for the express purpose of their enjoyment — now that was something to look forward to! She would bet all the money in her piggy bank that no other group of children had ever been singled out by someone as famous as Mr Von Gobstopper. Perhaps this momentous event might one day be featured in history books and be the cause of envy for students all over the globe. And if that was a little far-fetched, perhaps the fact that someone with an international profile had acknowledged their efforts would help dispel the suspicion that had followed Milli and Ernest of late. Milli inhaled deeply in an attempt to curb her excitement before she reached home but it would not be tamed. It bubbled inside her so fervently that she literally squirmed and wriggled her way through the front gate.

Milli's elder sister, Dorkus, was sitting in a cane chair on the front porch. It had taken months of coaxing by Rosie to get Dorkus to have an *outdoor* experience; however, persistence had paid off, even though Dorkus still refused to venture beyond the porch steps in case the house should float away and leave her behind while her back was turned. If anyone ever did suggest she move beyond the porch, Dorkus would launch into a hyena howl and cling obstinately to the veranda posts, causing even Stench to slink away in fear.

Milli's return from school was the highlight of Dorkus's day. During the hours that Milli was at school, Dorkus filled the time with reading, needlework, shelling peas and other sedentary activities. Occasionally, she watched the people in their street coming and going. She had an eye for detail and could tell you who had left their house at exactly what time and what they were wearing. Milli could imagine her sister running her own business one day: *Dorkus Investigations — No Stone Left Unturned*. Once she could be enticed to leave the house, that is.

As was their usual routine, Dorkus followed Milli indoors to exchange the news of the day.

'Mrs Nutcup went shopping with her wicker basket and came home with nothing but plums,' Dorkus informed Milli.

'Perhaps she's making jam,' Milli replied, feigning interest.

She dropped her satchel and rummaged quickly through the kitchen cupboards in search of a snack. Once she'd decided on some Wopple Juice and a plate of Nitty-Gritty Biscuits, she charged into the living room with Dorkus at her heels. Her parents were both there, heads together over the local paper and sharing a private joke.

'You both knew about this all the time!' Milli blurted. 'You knew and didn't say a word!' It wasn't a reprimand because at the same time she threw herself at her parents, hugging them so tightly that they struggled for breath.

'Well, we didn't want to spoil the surprise,' said Rosie.

'Your name's in the paper,' Milli told her. 'The headmaster read it out at assembly and everyone knew that my mother was involved. I was really proud. Do you need help with anything? I could help with dinner if you like.'

'Let's just say this cancels any planned trips to find the Fountain of Youth?' Rosie said with a wry smile.

'Deal,' agreed Milli.

Milli telephoned Ernest immediately after supper. The Perriclof family had recently installed a new Bakelite telephone as a concession to the advance of technology, but Milli rarely called as she knew the ringing unsettled

Mrs Perriclof's nerves. One of Ernest's siblings answered, using his best phone manner.

'Hello, Barabbas Perriclof speaking.'

'Hello, Bas,' Milli said. 'Is Ernest there, please?'

'This *is* Ernest,' Bas replied in a high-pitched squeal.

'Quit fooling around and put your brother on. Tell him it's Milli.'

'Milli who?' Bas asked cheekily. 'I'm sure Ernest doesn't know a Milli. You don't by any chance mean *Millipop*, do you?'

'I'm not going to ask you again,' Milli threatened. She could hear peals of laughter in the background and other little voices whispering together.

'Pop goes the weasel!' they shrieked before someone wrangled the phone from them.

Ernest apologised on behalf of his siblings and explained that they were probably *hyper* from eating too much roasted chickpea gelati. Milli wanted him to find Bas and spank him with a hairbrush but then remembered the purpose of her call.

'Can you believe it? I mean, it's such an amazing thing to happen. Who would have thought someone as important as Von Gobstopper would be interested in us! I simply can't wait for Friday!'

'How poor are they that have not patience,' Ernest replied.

'Ernest, please! I can't understand you when you speak like that.'

'Is the excursion the only thing we're going to talk about till Friday?' Ernest said sulkily.

'What else is there?' asked Milli.

'Have you finished your Chemistry homework? It's due tomorrow.' Milli was instantly deflated. 'There was Chemistry homework?' she said, and rang off.

The rest of the week was excruciatingly long for the Sparrows and Starlings of St Erudite's Academy. They tried their hardest to concentrate on school work and be deserving of the treat that was in store for them, but it wasn't easy. Every conversation found its way towards the subject of the imminent excursion. Milli drove Ernest mad with her incessant predictions of how the day might turn out. A poet had more important matters to think about. Toys were childish objects designed to occupy the minds of the very young. Whilst in principle Ernest had nothing against a little fun, he also remembered the consequences the last time the town allowed itself to indulge in what it believed to be harmless entertainment. But when he voiced his reservations to Milli, he found her enthusiasm could not be quelled.

'This is different,' she reasoned. 'Our parents and teachers are in on it, and, what's more, there's no one alive less like a villain than Von Gobstopper. You really need to relax, Ernie! Drink some more of that passionflower tea your mum's always brewing and try to stop being such a wet sock.'

'I think the expression is wet blanket and I'm not.'

'Fine,' Milli pouted. 'Just don't go spoiling things for the others. They have every right to be excited after everything they've been through.'

'Sorry,' mumbled a contrite Ernest.

Due to the number of students involved, it was decided that the excursion would be staggered over two days. On Friday morning, it was the first-formers who crowded around the school car park, all trying to get as close as possible to the door of the yellow bus in order to get on first and nab the prized back seats. Their animated chatter was relentless and the teachers accompanying them were already wincing in pain. The students were dressed in their dazzling best, having been permitted to be out of uniform for the day. They wore colourful beanies and jackets and carried little backpacks with packed lunches and clipboards should any note-taking be required. Most of the children had brought along their life savings (or as much of them as they had been permitted to withdraw) for the purchase of souvenirs. Milli had packed lightly, and swiftly disposed of her clipboard so as not to be weighed down during the tour of the arcade. Mrs Perriclof had packed Ernest's bag and every compartment was bursting with items that might come in handy. Milli spotted several thick spiral notebooks, a tin of coloured pencils, packets of tissues and throat lozenges, an extra pair of thick socks and a thermos of cream of asparagus soup.

Miss Macaw insisted the Sparrows form a civilised queue and ticked off names as they boarded the bus. 'Stop buzzing like bumblebees!' she cried. 'Stop chattering like chipmunks!' But she was smiling so they concluded she must understand, if not share, their excitement.

The trip to the arcade was a mere twenty minutes but this didn't stop the children from singing at the tops of their lungs as if they were heading off on a journey of several hours. They mostly sang one song, made up by a predecessor whose name had been forgotten. Parts of it made no sense at all but this did not, of course, detract from their pleasure in singing it. It was only the bus driver's face that turned purple in exasperation by the time they had run through it for the fourth time.

> *Oh, off we go — dippy-dee, dippy-doe,*
> *Bouncing on the ends of our tippy-tippy toes.*
> *Hungry little beavers — eager to see,*
> *Feeling dreadfully sorry for any absentees.*

We look up, we look down,
We look left and right and round,
Not a thing do we miss,
Not one Bruce or Dick or Chris.

All the other children are doing ordinary
  things,
While here in our bus we sit like kings
And now we're on our way!

As they sang they passed around bags of boiled sweets. Ernest munched on some roasted chestnuts that had turned as hard as pebbles. A boy called Ha-Ha Pyles shared his tin of blueberry marshmallows, which everyone had a try of. Ha-Ha Pyles was a sunny and good-natured boy despite his rather unfortunate surname. (Look it up if you think it doesn't sound too bad.) Ha-Ha was a nickname acquired from a habit of laughing at most things people said to him. You could say a casual 'It's looking like rain', or the slightly more sober 'My grandmother has just been diagnosed with dementia', and Peter's (his birth name) inevitable response was 'Ha-ha'. His teachers told his parents he would eventually outgrow the habit, and they were right; but the nickname stuck.

The singing stopped abruptly when the bus turned into a gravel driveway lined with poplars and pulled up in front of a magnificent construction that looked as if it had floated across the world from a Renaissance city. Milli and Ernest barely recognised the place that had once been their adoptive home. The twisting gravel drive was the only thing that had not been transformed. It seemed appropriate that what had once been a prison that repressed individual thought should now function as a place that celebrated childhood and enjoyment.

Von Gobstopper's Arcade had been modelled on the arcades found in many European cities. If you have ever seen one, you will know that they are tunnel-shaped buildings with arches for entrances, and a fair bit of decoration in the form of carved stone pillars, more arches and a dome of glass. Leading up to the entrance were hedges that had been shaped with bewitching artistry into giant toys. The children marvelled at a shrub teddy bear sitting on his bottom and waving his paws, two soldiers cut from poplars

81

that stood on either side of the entrance, and assorted gadgets such as yo-yos, bouncy balls and even a giant train set. Above the arched entrance, a painted daisy chain spelled out the words: *Von Gobstopper's Arcade — Children of All Ages Welcome.* Nearby, still outside, was a giant statue of the building's founder. Giant statues of founders or patrons usually look rather stern, but Von Gobstopper's statue showed a gentle, smiling man. He wore overalls, and was holding a hammer and a chisel, the most basic tools of his trade. Although he had a moustache, the crinkling around his eyes and the corners of his mouth indicated that he had never quite grown up.

Miss Macaw announced their arrival to a man in a ticket cubicle, but their presence had already been noted. She had barely finished speaking when there was a sound like the clashing of cymbals and an elegant woman in a smart suit, bubblegum pink, and with matching stilettos, appeared at the entrance and moved towards them with crisp and decisive gestures. She was inordinately tall and insect-thin. Her heels made a crunching sound on the gravel when she walked. Her face and hands were chalk white and her lips only slightly less pale. Her black hair was swept back from her oval face, smoothed into place by some unguent and held by tortoise-shell combs. The dark circles under her eyes suggested she was not a good sleeper. Although she could not be more than twenty, her demeanour suggested someone much older. Milli noticed that she didn't look directly at the children; rather, her eyes focused on an area slightly above their heads.

'Welcome to Von Gobstopper's Arcade,' she said in a tight and formal voice. 'My name is Ms Tempest Anomali and I am the curator.' She almost hissed as she emphasised her title. 'I will be conducting today's tour and there will be opportunities for questions later. The arcade comprises various levels, each one, as you shall see, dedicated to a special genre of toy or theme. But before we begin our adventure there are some important things you need to know, so I now request your full attention.'

The rules were few and simple, as Ms Tempest Anomali explained. The arcade was not a museum and interaction with the toys was invited. They must, however, behave respectfully at all times, as some of the items on display had travelled a long distance and were priceless. They could not wander away from the group at any time unless told otherwise, and they would be shown which shops it was possible to make purchases from. They must leave all bags and valuables in the cloakroom and the taking of photographs was strictly prohibited. Toys reacted badly to cameras flashing in their faces.

By the time the curator had finished her speech her expression had relaxed a little. She forced her mouth into a smile but it came out lopsided, as if this was the first time her lips had received such an instruction from her brain. 'Well, then,' she said, putting her palms together and inclining her head slightly, 'are we ready to go inside?'

She had not anticipated the eager cheer that followed. Her head jerked back and she suddenly looked affronted. But just as quickly her composure returned, along with the smile that looked more like a grimace, and she led the way inside.

CHAPTER SIX

Meeting Boi Toi

n order to convey to you the extent of the wonders the children were about to experience, I ask you to think about the most spectacular thing you have ever seen. Was it fireworks exploding like sea anemones across a midnight sky on New Year's Eve? Was it the costumes in a theatre production that were so vivid and lavish they took your breath away? Was it an architectural masterpiece viewed on a cultural tour with your parents? Whatever it was, think of your reaction magnified one hundred times and you may get some idea of how the children felt.

At first, however, there wasn't that much to

see — just a vast gallery with a richly coloured mosaic floor, decorative columns and quaint little shopfronts lining either side. Milli and Ernest observed immediately that the different levels within Hog House had been retained, forming tiers that reached upwards towards a domed ceiling made entirely of stained-glass panels that scattered beams of tinted light across the floor. There was a sweeping staircase to one side, and old-fashioned elevators, painted forest green, for those too impatient to climb the stairs.

The group stopped dutifully to read the arcade directory, which was shaped like an ancient scroll and held up by two brightly painted clay giants.

Between the giants' colossal sandalled feet was a map. Milli ignored it and instead tried to look inside the closest shops to determine their contents. At the entrance to one were giant powder puffs acting as revolving doors. It appeared to be a beauty parlour. What was a beauty parlour doing in the middle of a toy arcade, you may ask? Milli wondered the same thing and could only conclude that some of the

VON GOBSTOPPER'S
ARCADE DIRECTORY

This building is dedicated to childhood with all its dreams and fancies. Take your time in exploring it as every corner holds new surprises and visual delights. I hope that by the time you leave you will have reconnected with old friends and made some new ones.

Gustav Von Gobstopper

Basement Level
Not open to public
Ground Floor
Puppet Theatre, Clockworks Hall,
Toy Shoppe, Tearooms
Level One
A Doll's Life, Toys Through Time
Level Two
Teddies and other Furry Friends
Level Three
Transport and Construction Toys

toys availed themselves of such services. Another shop interior seemed to be choked with vegetation. Bulky vines hung from the ceiling and a carpet of leaves covered the floor. Milli was intrigued to see *Jungle Life* written on the plaque outside and in brackets below: *Unsupervised Entry Strictly Prohibited.*

The main gallery, where they were now standing, was lit by enormous gaslights held by wrought-iron arms protruding from the walls. A familiar and mouth-watering aroma filled the air. It smelled like a mixture of popcorn and vanilla biscuits. Ms Anomali pointed a thin finger to the ceiling, and when the children looked up, they nearly jumped out of their skins. Suspended on fishing wire above them was a row of teddy bears in tutus. They did a little choreographed dance and sang a welcome song; a performance which the children rewarded with riotous applause.

> *Welcome to the Toy Arcade*
> *A world filled with laughter.*
> *Make sure you've left your worries behind*
> *For there's no room for mopers.*

Welcome to the Toy Arcade
We hope you'll be enchanted.

Ms Anomali waited for the applause to subside then ushered them over to a pile of brightly coloured beanbags and indicated they should sit down. The children settled into the beanbags, which let out a 'Please sit down' in a range of different accents each time they adjusted their position, but fell silent when Ms Anomali began speaking.

'It is only when a toy loses its lustre of newness that it becomes really interesting,' the curator began. 'Many of the toy exhibits here are part of history. They all have a story to tell. I am sure you are already acquainted with the honey-coloured bear wearing a blue raincoat and red hat, or the wooden boy in overalls with the ridiculously long nose?' She spoke in such an alluring tone that her words sent shivers down their spines.

Looking down, Ernest noticed that the mosaic floor depicted characters and scenes from famous fairy stories. There was an ice castle, a knight in pursuit of a dragon and a princess with hair the colour of corn leaning out of a tower. He wondered how long it had taken to assemble such a collection of images. The attention to detail was remarkable. Tempest Anomali's velvet voice brought him back to the present.

'A word of warning. This arcade, although built for the entertainment of children, is vast and contains many rooms and passageways. It would not do for any of you to get lost. You cannot be sure what you may encounter, and some of the electronic toys are not easy to control. It is therefore imperative that you follow my instructions at all times. The basement level is strictly out of bounds as it contains dangerous machinery. We don't want to be sending anyone home minus a finger, do we?'

The knuckles of the curator's hands, which she'd clasped tightly in front of her throughout her talk, were white by the time she had finished and she wrinkled her nose as if there was a bad smell in the vicinity that she was having trouble identifying. Ms Anomali seemed about to announce the commencement of the tour when she was interrupted by a question. It came from

Ha-Ha Pyles, who hadn't been put off by her imperious manner. 'Is Mr Von Gobstopper himself likely to make an appearance at any stage of the day?' he asked eagerly.

A look somewhere between scorn and amusement flickered briefly over Tempest Anomali's chalky face.

'I'm afraid not,' she replied in dulcet tones. 'Mr Von Gobstopper is in retirement and rarely appears in public. It is too stressful for him; it interferes with his creative *chi*. You will, however, see evidence of his creativity in abundance! To begin, we hope you enjoy our dramatisation of the poem written for children by Christina Rossetti, "Goblin Market".'

A suspended platform, unnoticed by the children up to now, lit up. On it stood a toy theatre made of cardboard, high enough for everyone to see without craning their necks. Even though the characters were printed on cards attached to wooden sticks, and slid in and out of slots in the stage floor, the children were instantly engrossed in the story. It was a dramatic tale about two sisters, Laura and Lizzie, and their different reactions upon encountering goblin merchants selling some very enticing fruit. The children were relieved to see that sisterly devotion prevailed over the menacing goblins in the end, but everyone was left wondering what their decision might have been had they encountered such tempting merchandise on their way to fetch water.

When the show ended, the black-clad puppeteers, who had also provided the voices for all the characters, appeared in a row to take a bow.

'And now,' Ms Anomali announced, 'let us move on to the first exhibition, the Clockworks Hall. Here you will see a range of toys operated by the winding of some kind of key or mechanical device. Such toys were immensely popular with Victorian children — I believe they originated out of a human desire to bring inanimate things to life. Human beings are arrogant enough, after all, to believe that everything should mimic their own behaviour.'

She paused, seemingly in expectation of some reaction. Had she made a joke? The children wriggled uncomfortably until someone asked whether the toys had anything to do with clocks.

'Obviously they are thus named because their design employs similar principles to those employed in the making of clocks,' Ms Anomali replied coolly.

She turned sharply on her heels and marched down a nearby passageway. Feeling a mixture of anticipation and suspense, the children scurried after her. On their way they managed to read some of the plaques on the shopfronts: *Edible Building Blocks, Bath Friends, Golliwog Makeover, Barbie World, Planes 'n' Stuff.* The shop windows were in semi-darkness, keeping their wares well hidden.

Ms Anomali led them into a long, narrow hall where clockwork toys were displayed on low tables. Heavy curtains were drawn around a larger display stand in the centre of the hall. The children were invited to walk around freely to examine the toys on display. They could even operate them, as long as they did so one at a time.

The next half-hour was spent in gleeful exploration and the noise level grew steadily as various clockwork toys moved across the shiny floor displaying their particular skills. If you had previously said 'clockwork toy' to any of these children, they would have perhaps envisaged a soldier beating a drum. They now realised that the sky was the limit in the manufacture of such toys. Soon all manner of clockwork toys were buzzing around them like exotic insects. There were tiny birds that swarmed unexpectedly from mouse holes, pursued by motor-operated cats; battery-operated motorcycles transporting stylish dolls in bathing suits; pandas waving their paws in greeting; sumo wrestlers that twisted themselves into the most torturous positions; a nanny steering a baby in a perambulator; vampires that bared their teeth as they flew across the room; and monkeys that turned somersaults over and over. All the movements, although mechanical, were fluid and amazingly lifelike.

When Ms Anomali felt that they had seen enough, she pulled a lever on a panel and the toys clambered up onto the tables and resumed their stationary positions.

'Now,' the curator said, gliding over to the curtained display, 'it is time for something really special. This toy has been years in the making and once you meet him you'll understand why.

Have you ever seen a toy that can look you directly in the eye, tell jokes and play catch? Allow me to present to you, on loan to us all the way from Tokyo, Boi Toi.'

The heavy curtains fell away and there on a pedestal stood a mechanical boy roughly Ernest's size. He had jet black hair, a swatch of which fell over one eye, and skin the colour of milky coffee. The whites of his eyes were whiter than white and his cheeks were perfectly sculpted. His painted rosy lips were parted slightly in a smile.

Ms Anomali withdrew a remote control device from her breast pocket and pressed a button. Boi Toi's arm bent at the elbow with a slight scraping sound. The action revealed an enormous metal key jutting from his side. His narrow eyes blinked, the lashes brushing against porcelain skin. Slowly, he opened his mouth, the jaw detaching from the rest of his face like on a ventriloquist's dummy. Then the lips widened into a smile.

'My name is Boi Toi,' he said in a monotone. 'I am happy to make your acquaintance.'

He took a wonky step forward, which caused the children to take one back. Even the usually adventurous Miss Macaw had safely positioned herself behind Gummy Grumbleguts. Milli, who didn't want to appear overwhelmed so early in the day's preceedings, decided to take a step forward.

'He's not real,' she said. 'Look!'

She reached out bravely to stroke the waving mechanical hand. They had not, after all, been instructed not to touch. Immediately the clockwork toy's hand snapped shut around her wrist. Milli tried to shake her hand free but Boi Toi's grip was as strong as a vice. The class gasped as his shiny face bore down on her. Milli saw Boi Toi's eyes flash at her, so lifelike now they sent shivers up her spine, and he bared his teeth.

'He's just being friendly,' the curator reassured her. 'No harm done.'

She pushed another button and the toy released Milli's wrist. Milli moved away so quickly it caused Boi Toi to lurch forward. Ms Anomali was at his side with supernatural speed to catch him in case he fell. But he regained his balance unassisted and, smiling even more widely, parroted the words, 'No harm done.'

The curator punched a few more buttons and Boi Toi walked stiff-legged back to his stand and hoisted himself back up. 'Perhaps we may meet again,' he said vacantly before becoming immobile. The curtains swished shut, enshrouding him from view again.

'Unique, isn't he?' said Ms Anomali with undisguised affection.

No one replied.

In an attempt to defuse the tension created by Boi Toi's misconduct, Ms Anomali looked up at a spider clock suspended below the vaulted ceiling and announced it was time for morning tea, which would be served in the Teddy Bear Bakery.

'Don't worry,' she clucked, noting the wary expressions on some of the faces around her. 'Teddies are friendly.'

The Teddy Bear Bakery was an old-fashioned cosy tearoom on the ground floor. A tiered display in the window offered such delights as iced cakes sitting like monuments on silver platters, lamingtons so laden with cream and jam they wobbled, meringues in the shapes of cars and planes, and golden scones piled in a pyramid. The centrepiece was a giant pavlova with passionfruit oozing over a golden crust. Inside, there were checked tablecloths and spotted china. The children sat on upholstered chairs and were served by a team of teddy waitresses in pink aprons and hats who sped around on roller skates taking their orders.

Gummy Grumbleguts rather shocked Ms Anomali by declaring that he would have 'one of everything' until Miss Macaw whispered something tactfully in his ear and he announced sheepishly that he was only joking.

Morning tea was followed by a whirlwind tour of so many different exhibits the children wondered how they would remember them all. Ernest, assiduous as ever, made notes on everything they saw and also did some impromptu sketches in anticipation of the follow-up activities they might be given back at school. Milli, of course, decided that note-taking would only interfere with her appreciation of what she was seeing and decided that she would rely on memory (and Ernest's copious notes if he could be bribed into sharing them) should there be some major assignment awaiting them on Monday.

In Perambulator Place, prams made of the finest silk held infant dolls so lifelike they cried in response to noise of any kind and sucked on their rubbery thumbs. They visited a shop that gave off a distinct odour of emergency (if you have never smelled an emergency it is a sort of metallic scent with a hint of wood smoke and whisky). Inside this shop figurines of all of history's superheroes were mounted on the walls, from Wonder Puss to Volcano Man. When the curator tugged at a cord behind each figure's shoulders, they sprang to life and zoomed around the room, shouting catchphrases like *I'll save you* and *Have no fear, help is here!* At one point, several superheroes joined forces to lift the smallest member of their class, Titchy Le Piccolo, right off his feet. Next the children visited the shop Milli had already peered into, where it seemed as if an entire forest had sprung up from the floor. They heard a strange snuffling then stuffed animals burst from all directions. Monkeys swung down from the vines, metallic snakes slithered from beneath bushes, and toucans squawked in the branches of the trees.

In a shop called Farm Yard Friends they found sheep bleating, pigs grunting and horses whinnying in their various enclosures. In The Golliwog Tree, the entire space was filled with tree branches displaying gollies of all shapes and sizes. Golliwogs are so engaging they don't have to *do* anything, and there was something very endearing about their button eyes and crimson smiles that made this one of the children's favourite stops.

Their next visit was to a large room draped in velvet and lit by ornate lamps on side tables. Those easily frightened were warned beforehand to wait outside as this room might hold some sudden shocks. No one took up the offer. The shop was called Haunted Chairs, and spread around its interior was a collection of chairs like assorted chocolates in a box. They ranged from a shabby low stool to a deep armchair upholstered in a cabbage rose design. The curator explained that each chair was inhabited by a character that only came to life once someone sat in the chair.

After considerable deliberation, Gummy Grumbleguts offered to go first. He chose the small, inoffensive-looking stool, concluding that it couldn't pose too much of a threat. As soon as he sat down, the notes of a harp filled the air and the stool, with Gummy atop it, sailed gracefully across the room and back. Milli tried the armchair, but quickly regretted her decision because a cabbage rose on the arm reconfigured into the face of an old witch, warty and as wrinkled as a prune. The witch hissed and glared at the terrified onlookers and her skinny arms reached right out of the chair in an attempt to catch hold of a child. Milli tried to leap up immediately but couldn't move until the witch's arms and face dissolved once more into the flower pattern. Ernest decided to take his chances with a sea captain's chair. No sooner had he sat down than the menacing bald heads of four pirates emerged from each leg and threatened to make him walk the plank if he didn't immediately empty the contents of his pockets.

Their next stop was, thankfully, more sedate. The sign outside read: *Thimble Sisters — Doll*

Dressmakers since 1864. The children were instructed not to make any noise or ask questions during this visit as the dressmakers were involved in work that required absolute concentration. The sisters, Ethel and Eve, were elderly women, delicate and fine-boned, who sat on a raised platform and were so engrossed in their craft they barely acknowledged the children's entrance. The room they worked in was small and circular, and every inch of it was cluttered with tiny rolls of fabric, lacquered sewing boxes and tubes of sequins and glitter. One sister was sewing pearls onto a tiny ballgown whilst the other crocheted a mantle in gold thread. So skilful were they that they didn't need to keep their eyes on their handiwork but instead gazed into the distance, in all likelihood dreaming of romance.

CHAPTER SEVEN

A Message in the Snow

xciting as all the displays were, nothing prepared Milli and Ernest for what happened during their tour of the first floor. This floor, as you may recall from the directory, was where dolls and their paraphernalia were located. Glass cabinets along the main walkway displayed rare dolls in all their finery, too fragile or too valuable to be handled by inquisitive hands. Striking as these were, most children gave them only a fleeting glance, so intent were they on discovering the contents of the individual shops. The dolls were all exquisite, with radiant eyes, flawless complexions and heart-shaped mouths the

103

colour of the glacé cherries found in Christmas cakes. Some displays centred around specific themes, and one of the most lavish was called: *A White Christmas for Gwendolyn and Friends*. This charming scene had been assembled with the utmost attention to detail, from the crisp folds in the dolls' dresses to the powdery snowflakes that fell in little mounds at their feet. Tiny presents were scattered around a decorated tree. Gwendolyn and her friends were dressed smartly in fur-trimmed navy capes and lace-up boots and arranged as if enjoying various snow-related activities. Two were busy constructing a snowman, others were rather recklessly skating on a pond that had frozen over, whilst Gwendolyn herself (easily identified by the finery of her dress) was stepping into a sleigh for a ride around the park. Dozens of glass eyes stared at Milli and Ernest.

'Funny how if you stare long enough, you start to believe they're looking back,' Milli commented.

'They are very lifelike,' Ernest agreed, and they both hurried on to catch up with the others.

It was then that the peculiar thing happened, and it happened, as most peculiar things do, quite by chance. When Ernest went to write down some historical fact Ms Anomali was telling them, he realised he had dropped his pencil. He ran back to look for it and found it, as expected, on the floor just in front of the snow display that he and Milli had stopped to admire. He bent to retrieve it and, giving the display a final glance, saw that something was different. He was sure that the main doll, Gwendolyn, had changed position. He was almost certain she had been standing alongside the sleigh the last time he looked. He looked more closely, and saw the imprint of tiny feet making a track through the snow. He followed the path and saw that someone had written a cryptic message in the snow in the foreground of the display. The letters were fine enough to have been made by the tip of Gwendolyn's parasol; there was no other implement in the snowscape that could be responsible. He pressed his nose up against the display case and saw that the letters spelled out a phrase in a language he could not immediately identify: ꟼƧƨ ᴟ . On the glass right beside Ernest's nose he thought he could see a tiny handprint, as if a doll's hand had momentarily rested there. And when he looked at the dolls' faces he imagined he saw something more than a glassy façade; he thought he saw a real and unaccountable sadness. The moment lasted only a second — interrupted by a call for Ernest to rejoin the group — but a second was enough for Ernest's mind to click into top gear. When he looked at the letters again, he didn't see a puzzle but a cry for help. For the letters were upside down and back to front. Positioned the right way they read: *help us*.

As Ernest rejoined his classmates, he felt an icy hand clutch his shoulder. He jumped.

'Young man,' Ms Anomali scolded, 'are you aware that you have been holding up the entire group? If we don't get a move on we won't be able to see everything.'

'The doll, Gwendolyn …' Ernest began rather helplessly, but stopped before he could say anything utterly absurd.

'Yes, she's very attractive,' Ms Anomali continued for him, 'but I'm afraid it's not an attachment that shows the least bit of promise.'

Some children tittered at this but Ernest just

looked blankly up at the curator. It made Milli want to hug him. Only much later did it occur to the two children that Ms Anomali was trying to deflect attention from the snowscape display.

'What's going on?' Milli quizzed Ernest during the lunch break.

'I don't know. I can't explain it because I'm not sure it makes sense.'

'Can you show me?'

They made their way back to the exhibit and both scrutinised the scene behind the glass. Everything was as it had been upon first viewing. The dolls were rigidly in position and the scrawled message had disappeared. The artificial snow lay on the ground so neatly each flake might have been individually positioned.

'Sorry, I don't get it,' Milli said finally.

'It's gone,' Ernest replied flatly.

'What's gone?'

Ernest rattled off the previous events in quick succession, in case they were suddenly intercepted.

'There was a message before — *help us* — in the snow and now it's gone. It could only have come from one of the dolls — Gwendolyn, I think. I'm sure it was meant for *us*.'

What happened next cemented Milli's and Ernest's friendship for at least the next five years. Milli didn't roll her eyes, smirk or do anything else that remotely suggested she doubted Ernest. In fact, she responded as if his assertion was the most normal thing in the world.

'So what do we do now?'

'Not sure. We need to think. After all, they stumble that run fast.'

'Yes,' agreed Milli, 'and they get clobbered that speak in riddles.'

'We don't have much time,' Ernest said. 'Let's see if anything else happens.'

'Not much chance of that. That curator person seems to have eyes at the back of her head.'

'There's bound to be another break at some point. We'll have a good look around then.'

An opportunity presented itself mid-afternoon, when the children were given time to browse the toy shops on the ground floor. Miss Macaw's instructions were clear: they were free to wander until 2:55 pm, when they were to meet at the arcade's entrance in order to catch the bus back to St Erudite's. Milli and Ernest slowly distanced themselves from the group and crept up to level one. The silence was eerie without the velvety commentary from the curator. They returned to the dolls in the snow and Milli even tapped lightly on the glass case.

'Hello, in there. Blink if you can understand me.'

'Shut up, Milli. Someone might hear us.'

The children wandered aimlessly through the gallery, not sure of what exactly they ought to be looking for. Time seemed to stand still as they became engrossed in displays they'd been rushed past earlier. When they finally looked over the balcony to the floor below it was empty. With pounding hearts they charged down the stairs and froze in horror. The cloakroom too was empty, and the only thing in the gravel driveway was a magpie picking relentlessly at something lodged between the pebbles. The yellow school bus carrying their classmates had gone.

'Don't panic,' said Milli. 'They'll be back as

soon as they realise.'

'Miss Macaw must have forgotten to do a head count.'

'What bad luck. Should we wait here or keep looking?' Milli asked.

Ernest didn't get a chance to answer because just then they heard the familiar sound of Ms Anomali's heels tapping on the mosaic floor. It sounded exactly like twigs snapping. She was heading outside, right where they were standing.

They hid behind some shrubbery growing against the arcade wall but it barely concealed them. Any moment now she would find them and then there would be real trouble. The last thing St Erudite's needed was bad publicity after Von Gobstopper's generous gift to the school. They could just see the headlines now: ERRANT CHILDREN CAUGHT TRESPASSING! Then, just as Ms Anomali's steps changed to a crunching as she reached the gravel, they heard a different sound. It seemed to be coming from behind the wall they had flattened themselves against in their attempt to become invisible.

'Psst!' a voice said urgently. 'Get inside,

quick! Before she sees you!' An opening appeared in the stone wall at around knee-height. Without thinking, Milli and Ernest ducked inside. They found themselves standing in a damp and poorly lit passageway. They looked around to see who had rescued them but nobody was there.

'Down here,' the voice said, making them both jump.

It was coming from ground level, and when they looked down they saw a little toy soldier wearing a red military jacket. He gave them a salute and clicked his heels. Now that he had their attention he was beaming all over his little wooden face.

'Fear not, little miss,' the toy soldier said, 'my name is Captain Pluck and I have come to guide you to safety.' His eyes wandered to Ernest's rucksack. 'And you, young master, I see, have come prepared.'

The children stared at him with mouths agape. Ernest blinked several times in an effort to clear his vision. He knew he wasn't hallucinating because he saw on Milli's face the same expression he imagined to be on his own. Toys weren't meant to speak — they were inanimate objects. Even the breathtakingly lifelike toys created by Gustav Von Gobstopper were still only toys. If they could communicate at all it was in mechanical and toneless greetings.

Milli's initial amazement started to pass and she looked at the soldier with more curiosity than shock, as if some secret theory she had harboured all her life had just been confirmed.

'Did you …' Ernest began, and faltered. 'I'm sure you didn't just …'

'Speak up, lad!' the soldier demanded. 'What are you jabbering about?'

Both children jumped upon hearing the voice again. There was no denying that it had come from Captain Pluck. They could see his lips moving, and not in an unnatural way but almost as the mouth of a human might move when speaking. In fact, the toy was staring at them as if he found their behaviour quite strange.

'We beg your pardon … err … Captain Pluck,' Milli began, realising he was waiting for an answer from them. 'We don't mean to be rude, it's just that we've never met a talking toy before. You took us by surprise.'

Now it was the soldier's turn to look surprised. 'Never met a toy who could talk?' he said incredulously. 'Did you think we were all mute dummies? Surely your own special toys at home have acquired the ability of speech?'

'Not as yet,' Milli answered.

'Slow developers then,' said Captain Pluck, shaking his head. 'Perhaps you haven't provided them with sufficient stimulation.' He became suddenly thoughtful as he eyed the children up and down. 'How did you come to be loitering outside the arcade on your own?'

Ernest didn't like his suspicious tone. 'We were left behind by accident when we went to investigate an SOS,' he said.

The soldier brightened suddenly. 'An SOS? Why didn't you say so! You had better come and meet the others.'

'The others?' echoed Ernest but the soldier was no longer listening.

'Hurry along and follow me now. There's no time to lose.'

Captain Pluck turned on his heel and

113

marched off down the passageway ahead, which was rather narrow and more like a tunnel. Milli and Ernest hesitated a moment. They had no doubt that their absence would soon be noticed and the school bus (carrying a distraught Mildew Macaw) would return to collect them. But that might take a little time — perhaps, if they hurried, just enough time to follow this extraordinary little toy and learn more about the inhabitants of the arcade.

CHAPTER EIGHT

Toys Underground

The tunnel wasn't designed to accommodate children and Milli and Ernest had to walk with bowed heads. It was just as well Milli had routinely fed her vegetables to a not-so-finicky Stench at dinner, or she might well have grown too big to get through.

After several minutes of travelling along the cramped passageway, the toy soldier looked up at the children. 'Is everything all right, Miss? Not too uncomfortable, I hope?'

It took Milli a moment to realise he was speaking to her. He reached up to guide her with his tiny wooden hand. 'Just say the word and I shall carry you all the way! I know the underground is not an easy place for a young lady. Let me know if you need to rest.'

When, minutes later, a thud followed by a yelp indicated that Ernest had hit his head on the roof of the tunnel, Captain Pluck was less sympathetic. 'Try to keep your wits about you, man,' he called out, without so much as a backward glance. 'The enemy can come at you anytime and from anywhere.'

After what seemed like a long time of semi-stumbling in the dark, they emerged into an underground chamber. Finally they were able to stand up and stretch their stiff necks. They looked around. There were some faded maps taped to one wall and a couple of camp beds. On a bench stood what looked like a radio with wires hanging in a tangle from its sides, and an old-fashioned spyglass. There was also a round table with four low stools. On one of these sat a gruff-looking teddy bear wearing a bandana. On another was propped the most beautiful ballerina doll they had ever laid eyes on.

It was the doll who spoke first. She leapt from her stool and, balancing on the tips of her

116

shoes, whirled over to the newcomers at such speed that her tutu resembled the blades of a blender in action. Up close the children could see that her ballet slippers were embroidered with stars and cream ribbons curled their way up her shapely legs. Her curly golden mane was swept up into an elaborate knot at the nape of her neck and studded with pink and white rosebuds. Some curls had escaped and hung rather limply on her cheek. A glittering tiara sat atop the concoction of curls. Her wide eyes were as deep and as blue as the ocean. She had petite features and very long lashes that swept her cheeks when she blinked. She fluttered them now as she approached the children. Milli noticed that the tulle of her tutu was looking a bit on the crumpled side, her tiara was crooked and her leotard had a streak of mud down one side.

'My name is Pascal,' the doll announced importantly. 'Did you by any chance happen to bring a mirror with you?'

'No, we didn't,' said Milli, thinking it a very strange question. 'Seeing as we didn't plan on coming at all.'

'What about a comb?' Pascal said, looking hopefully at Ernest's backpack.

'That I am never without,' said Ernest, eager to oblige.

Pascal took Ernest's oversized comb, which looked like a rake in her hands, and her face fell. 'My hair is a disaster — full of knots.'

'Perhaps I could help?' suggested Ernest.

'Oh, would you? I would be ever so grateful. Did you notice that my nail varnish has chipped? Tell me the truth — you did notice, didn't you?' Pascal dropped the comb, put her face in her hands and burst into a flood of tears.

Milli and Ernest didn't know quite how to react but the burly teddy bear seemed accustomed to such outbursts.

'Now, now, Pascal,' he chided gently. 'Let's not alarm our visitors before we have even had a chance to be properly introduced.' On two feet, the bear was the largest teddy the children had ever come across, reaching well above their knees. He patted Pascal paternally on the head whilst watching the children intently. 'Pascal has had the hardest time adapting to life underground,' he explained. 'Her previous home

118

was a French chateau, specially designed for her, full of mirrors and an extensive wardrobe. She misses her old life.'

'I wasn't made to be a soldier!' the doll wailed.

Milli thought she seemed a very shallow and selfish sort of character even though the bear was clearly sorry for her.

The bear introduced himself as Theo. Up close they could see that he was a rich amber colour, with eyes to match, although some patches of fur on his arms looked a little frayed. The black bandana around his forehead was fastened in a knot at the back. He wore a battered leather jacket and a pair of sandshoes. Somewhere along the way he seemed to have done away with his pants, but was totally unself-conscious about it and retained an innate dignity. In fact, he had a streetwise look about him and if he were human he'd probably have been a bouncer or a musician in a jazz band. He clearly had some authority within the group because Pascal fell silent at his touch. She sniffed back her tears and tried to look stoic but only succeeded in looking up at Theo like a petulant child who is making an effort to be good. The bear turned his attention to the children.

'Where did you come from?' he asked.

Seeing that the children hadn't sufficiently recovered from their surprise to reply, Captain Pluck answered on their behalf.

'Castaways,' he whispered, 'from the *excursion*.'

'Ah, the excursion,' Theo said. 'We've been hoping to meet you. It's Milli and Ernest, isn't it?'

'How do you know that?' asked a baffled Ernest.

'Let's just say your reputation has preceded you. We,' he made a sweeping gesture with his arm — 'are the Resistance.'

'What's a resistance?' Milli asked innocently.

'You'll have to forgive my friend,' Ernest cut in, frowning at Milli. 'She never pays enough attention in History. I know that a resistance is a secret organisation set up to oppose an enemy occupation.'

Theo smiled. 'You *do* pay attention, I see.'

'The question is, whom or what are you resisting?'

Ernest's little speech may have annoyed

Milli, but Theo broke into a roar of laughter and extended a furry paw to shake Ernest's hand.

'Someone with your thinking is going to be immensely useful to us. But tell me, how did you come to be left behind?'

'We think a doll in one of the displays tried to send Ernest a message,' Milli replied, anxious not to be completely excluded from the conversation. 'He saw *help us* written in the snow but we don't know who wrote it or why.'

The bear nodded. 'I was afraid it was a long shot, but we had to try everything to get your attention. Thankfully, you have proved as observant as I had hoped.'

'It *was* intended for us,' said Ernest, still struggling to get things clear in his head. 'I knew it!'

'Of course,' the bear rumbled. 'We are in desperate need of friends.'

'Perhaps you could explain to us what's going on?' asked Milli politely. 'We are, as Ernest would say, a tad confused.'

'And we don't have much time,' Ernest thought it wise to add, 'before the bus comes back to collect us.'

'Please sit down,' said Theo, 'and I'll try to be as brief as I can. Afterwards, you can decide whether you wish to be of assistance or not.'

The bear sat down on his stool, took a deep breath and exhaled slowly as he considered how to make his explanation as succinct as possible.

'It is not possible to tell you everything right now,' he began, 'so I'll try to focus on the important bits. The three of us have been friends for a long time. We formed part of our maker's special collection. The first thing I imagine you're wondering is why we can use speech whilst others can't?'

The children nodded encouragingly.

'Well, that part is not so easy to explain. I could say it was due to magic, but that wouldn't be quite correct, although magic has no doubt played a part in it, just not the magic you are accustomed to. No, it is more the magic of creative endeavour. When Von Gobstopper created us, he imbued each of us with a specific identity and human qualities. As toys are Von Gobstopper's only companions, he creates them

122

to resemble humans — not in appearance but in personality.'

'Does this mean all Von Gobstopper's toys can speak?' Milli asked breathlessly.

'I doubt it, although we think they may have the capacity to learn. We were fortunate enough to form part of Von Gobstopper's inner circle and our creator certainly has a taste for debate.' The bear paused and chuckled, clearly enjoying some private reminiscence. 'Eventually, we learned to answer him when he posed philosophical questions. He was delighted with his achievement, of course. We all became firm friends.'

'How do you explain the message in the display?' Milli interrupted.

'Gwendolyn is special, and far too accomplished to spend her life as a prop in a display,' Theo muttered in anger. 'Sadly, she became trapped in a glass enclosure with companions she cannot communicate with. Hopefully, it will not be forever.'

'We've read that Mr Von Gobstopper is now a recluse,' commented Ernest, keen to keep the discussion from straying.

'Recluse!' snorted Captain Pluck. 'Is that what they call it? Hostage, more like!'

'Calm down, Pluck,' said Theo. 'We're still trying to determine what happened to him.' He turned back to the children. 'We travelled here by coach, a whole party of us, including Von Gobstopper and a number of his staff, for the opening of the arcade. But on the way we were intercepted and Von Gobstopper has not been seen since.'

'So how come you're living down here?' Milli asked.

'We are not living here,' the bear corrected her kindly, 'we are in *hiding*. The worst part is that we don't know exactly what we are hiding from. The arcade has been taken over. We escaped as soon as we suspected something was wrong — before we could be locked away as part of an exhibit.'

'What makes you think anything is wrong at all?' said Ernest. 'Is it possible that Mr Von Gobstopper has just gone home and put others in charge of running the arcade?'

'That would be an entirely plausible conclusion if we didn't know Mr Von Gobstopper better,' Theo reflected.

124

'He would never abandon us!' Captain Pluck said indignantly.

'Something is very wrong,' added Pascal, tearing up again.

Theo gave the children a serious look. 'We're hoping you'll help us determine what that something is.'

They were interrupted by the crunch of wheels on gravel, audible even in the Resistance's underground headquarters.

'The bus!' exclaimed Ernest.

'Captain Pluck will escort you out,' Theo announced. 'We don't want to cause you any more trouble. Please come and see us again soon if you can.'

'How do we let you know we're coming?'

'There's no need. We'll know when you get here. Wait at the opening in the wall and use the password.'

'But we don't know the password,' Milli said.

'Of course you don't; how remiss of me. It's Peppered Pancakes.'

Ernest had already shouldered his pack, keen to return to the driveway and the bus in the hope that a rapid return might lessen the scolding they were bound to receive from Miss Macaw. Milli, however, the more instinctive of the pair, sensed there was something the toys were holding back.

'Is there anything else you can tell us?' she asked. 'Anything else not quite right?'

'There is one thing,' the bear said hesitantly. He stole a glance at the others to ensure he had their approval to proceed. They gave almost imperceptible nods.

'On three occasions now there has been what we call a "round-up" in the arcade,' he told them, 'during which certain toys are taken down to the basement for repairs. Perhaps five or six at a time.'

'What's strange about that?' asked Ernest. 'Toys must need maintenance.'

Theo fixed him with a grim look.

'That is true, Ernest, we do. Only in these instances not a single toy taken for maintenance has ever come back.'

CHAPTER NINE

A Bond is Forged

When Milli awoke safe and sound in her own bed the next morning, she wondered what was causing the feeling of unease in the pit of her stomach. Then she remembered the events of the day before. Luckily, Miss Macaw had been too relieved that they hadn't been dismembered by Boi Toi or abducted by stuffed jungle animals to ask many questions. Milli and Ernest had simply invented a story about wandering off to take more detailed notes and losing track of time, and everyone believed them. It sounded just like something the conscientious Ernest would do. Besides, no one could imagine deliberately staying behind to risk incurring the wrath of the venomous Ms Anomali. At times during the tour, the curator's expression had suggested that nothing would give her more satisfaction than to see the visitors pickled in a jar.

Milli and Ernest had agreed with Theo not to publicise their meeting and they fended off the queries from the other students, eager to hear what they had got up to. Both children were equally reticent when they returned home. They remained so all through dinner, which surprised their parents who had expected them to be brimming with stories about the arcade.

'Too much glitz and not much substance,' was Ernest's rather dismissive report.

Mr and Mrs Perriclof attributed their first-born's non-communication to him entering the uncharted waters of adolescence, something they had long been dreading. They had been warned by well-meaning friends that Ernest's conversation would soon be reduced to a series of incomprehensible grunts. Change of any sort was not well received in the Perriclof household. Mrs Perriclof's solution (as it was for most of life's tricky situations) was to increase Ernest's

Vitamin B intake and rush him off to a yoga class.

Mrs Klompet, on the other hand, simply concluded that as Milli was so quiet she must be over-tired or coming down with something and advised an early night. Only Dorkus realised that her sister was neither ill nor tired. She had noticed Milli chewing compulsively on her lower lip; something she only ever did when she was hatching a devious plan or pondering a matter of the utmost importance.

Saturday turned out to be busy for both Milli and Ernest and they didn't find an opportunity to meet to discuss the events at the arcade. Ernest was flat out with rehearsals for *Macbeth* despite the paucity of his lines, and Milli had agreed to help her ever-inventive father trial a new pre-mixed Christmas pudding that, instead of the usual ingredients, contained pistachios and pumpkin. On Sunday afternoon it rained steadily and both the Klompets and the Perriclofs insisted their children stay indoors. Milli divided her time between checking the weather and playing a game of Hide and Seek with Stench as no one was willing to brave the rain to take him for his walk. You had to feel sorry for him, lying with his nose between his paws by the door and looking up hopefully every time someone walked past. The game involved a member of the family (usually Dorkus) covering Stench's eyes with her hands as she counted to ten. Then Dorkus would remove her hands and give the instruction, 'Find Milli!' Stench sprang into action and did a perfunctory lap of whatever room he happened to be in before bounding off to look for Milli. He always found her inside of sixty seconds, either behind the shower curtain, curled inside the blanket box or behind one of the coats hanging from the hall stand.

'Ten seconds,' announced Dorkus, checking her watch.

'Shame there isn't a *Guinness Book of Records* for animals,' said Milli as she rewarded the dog with a scratch behind his woolly ears. 'Or you'd be famous.'

When Monday came and the children sat on the school bus they felt quite disappointed with themselves for having achieved so little. Milli proposed that they return to the arcade after school that afternoon to find out more and see how the toys were faring, but Ernest wasn't convinced. He argued that there was little sense in acting rashly; what they really needed was time to think things through. They were supervised carefully at school and no one was at liberty to wander off willy-nilly. Getting caught breaking the rules was a different matter now that they were in senior school. He felt certain that those in authority would be less forgiving now, and any misdemeanours could have damaging consequences. Perhaps even lead to the loss of future positions of responsibility.

On the other hand, Milli reminded Ernest, they had to do *something*. And if they could agree on what that something was, it would be better decided upon sooner rather than later in case things changed suddenly at the arcade and they could no longer gain access to the secret passage.

The second excursion group was milling excitedly around the courtyard when the school bus pulled up. Watching them, Milli suddenly was struck by an idea.

131

'I've just had a great idea,' she announced.

'Really? Did it hurt?'

Milli held Ernest in a headlock until he took back the comment and agreed to listen.

'Make it quick,' he said, spotting teachers moving towards the common room for their first of many coffees for the day.

Milli outlined her plan in a low and urgent whisper. 'We can smuggle ourselves onto the bus and get back to the arcade that way. Then, as soon as we can, we'll wander off to spend the day with the toys. We won't even be missed because we're officially not there. And since today's group have to wear school uniform we'll blend in perfectly. Admit it … it's good.'

'The plan *is* good,' Ernest had to concede, 'apart from a few glitches — such as, how do we get on the bus if we're not on today's list?'

'A detail, my dear Ernesto. It's Mr Beaker taking this group, remember? He'll have forgotten he's even going and someone will have to go and find him. By that time we'll be on the bus with the others. When he takes the roll, he won't even realise there are two extras on board.'

'What if he does a head count?'

'He won't. He can't concentrate for that long.'

'What about the fact that we won't be in class all day?'

'I'll run up right now, get our names ticked off and say we need time in the library to write up Friday's outing for the newsletter. Teachers love students showing initiative.'

'Won't they expect to see the article?'

'That should take you all of ten minutes tonight.'

'Um, no, it'll take *us* all of ten minutes tonight,' Ernest amended.

'OK, but I doubt it'll take ten minutes if I help,' said Milli with a grin. 'So are we going?'

Ernest looked uncertain, and clutched his satchel which Milli was trying to wrestle from him. She planned to deposit it in the shrubbery where hers was already concealed. 'It seems a rash and poorly thought through plan, as well as involving the telling of several blatant lies which I'm not entirely comfortable with,' Ernest pointed out. But Milli was already gleefully bounding off to find Miss Macaw.

133

'But why let that stop us?' he concluded to himself.

If there was one thing Milli had observed about teachers it was that they loved to bask in reflected glory. Miss Macaw was no exception and was 'tickled pink' by the idea of a piece written by two of her students making it into the newsletter. She waved Milli off, supposedly to the library, her eyes already distant as she imagined the article being read by the entire school community, with the words 'Macaw Sparrows' beneath the authors' names.

Even the best of plans rarely unfold without some hiccup, but when one does it is immensely satisfying for the planners. Milli and Ernest were soon seated on the yellow school bus without so much as a challenge from even the most observant of the second-formers. They were too wrapped up in their own excitement to even consider the possibility of illegal passengers.

As the bus pulled into the sweeping drive and chugged its way to the arcade entrance, Milli was again struck by how ornate the building looked, rising up out of nowhere. On the way the children had considered the problem of being recognised by the curator, so they breathed a huge sigh of relief when the person who came out to greet the second group was someone entirely different. He introduced himself as Fritz Braun, one of Von Gobstopper's trainees. He spoke with a slight accent and a clipped tone that suggested English was not his mother tongue. There was a stiffness and formality about him that belied his years, for Fritz Braun could not have been more than seventeen or eighteen years old. He had coarse barley-coloured hair, cropped short, and skin so fair that light seemed to emanate from him. He had a straight Grecian nose and eyes shaped like half-moons that shone like pieces of sky in his severe face. He was tall, with broad arms and a thickish neck, and stood as straight as an ironing board with his arms bent at the elbows and legs slightly apart, as if prepared to leap into combat at any moment. For some of the children, this stance was a little unnerving, but a more perceptive observer might have realised that Fritz Braun was ill at ease. His clothes were odd — a shapeless sand-coloured tunic worn over a pair of loose-fitting pants and belted at the waist. The young man looked positively medieval.

'Wonder where Cruella is today?' Milli whispered to Ernest as they aimed for front row seats in front of the puppet theatre, as enthusiastic to see the performance as they had been the first time.

'Luckily for us, off duty,' Ernest replied.

Fritz seemed to relax a little as time wore on and soon proved himself a much more animated tour guide than Ms Anomali. He seemed to take genuine delight in observing the children's reactions. It was interesting, Milli and Ernest noted, that Boi Toi didn't make an appearance this time round, and they wondered whether he had required repairs after his malfunction. Fritz didn't bore them with a string of facts, instead relying on lively anecdotes to engage his audience. For example, while visiting a display on the second floor called Teddies at Work, which showed a selection of hefty teddies in construction hats operating various bits of machinery, he told them a story about how the teddy bear got its name. According to Fritz (who seemed an authoritative source) there was once an American president whom everyone liked to call Teddy. Teddy was a soft-hearted man who couldn't bring himself to shoot a bear cub on a hunting expedition. The event came to public attention when it appeared as a cartoon in the local press. Not long after, an enterprising shop-owner fashioned a soft toy based on the bear cub that Teddy could not shoot and dubbed it Teddy's Bear.

'The teddy evolved to become the most prized item in most children's toy collections,' concluded Fritz. 'In fact, research shows that the teddy has the special honour of being the one toy children are most reluctant to part with once they move on to other forms of recreation. It is the toy least likely to be passed on to younger siblings.'

He held the gaze of his audience as if challenging anyone to disagree. Nobody did. Ernest tried to look sceptical but Milli knew he was bluffing. She'd seen his Carpenter Ted, complete with leather apron and a pocket full of hammers and chisels, tucked away for future progeny.

Milli found Fritz's explanations enthralling; he was the sort of storyteller who appeared to be talking to every member of his audience individually. She liked Fritz so much that she might have been lured into taking the entire tour again had she not noticed, as she stopped again to admire the snowscape on the first floor, that the doll called Gwendolyn appeared to be frowning at her in disapproval. Milli and Ernest were certain this hadn't been the expression on her alabaster face the last time they saw her and it served as a reminder to them of their purpose in returning to the arcade. They chose an opportune moment when the teachers' energies were flagging and everyone was thinking about morning tea to slip away unnoticed.

Outside, they flattened themselves against the wall where they thought the opening to the secret passage was. 'Peppered Pancakes,' Milli whispered as loudly as she dared. Several moments passed and they thought they'd got the wrong spot, but then several stone blocks shifted and slid inwards to reveal the passageway. They crawled through on hands and knees, and found Theo waiting for them with a lantern swinging from one paw. They could tell from the expression in his clear brown eyes that he was relieved to see them.

'Wasn't sure you'd come,' he said hurriedly, 'but very glad you did. We can now think of you as friends of the Resistance.'

When their eyes had adjusted to the darkness the children saw that a train made up of open carriages had come to collect them. Each was the size of a small wheelbarrow. They were glad that they wouldn't have to walk the whole way doubled over. Their necks still hadn't quite recovered from last time. A plastic conductor in a bright blue uniform shouted 'All aboard' and they climbed into a carriage each, the children sitting cross-legged to fit. The train moved off down the narrow tunnel.

'The others will be pleased to see you,' Theo told them. 'They've not stopped talking about you.'

When Milli and Ernest scrambled out of the train into the subterranean hideout, Pascal's tiny face lit up and she pirouetted for a full thirty seconds in delight. Captain Pluck stepped forward smartly and clicked his heels in greeting.

'There's someone else we'd like you to meet,' Theo said, looking around. From the shadows emerged an elegant rocking horse the colour of crème brûlée. He was obviously an antique and the finest materials had been used in his construction. He had a leather harness and a mane of real horsehair. His bridle was red and his saddle made of calfskin. He had a broad back and sturdy haunches, and his rockers were glossy and black.

'This is Loyal,' the bear went on as the horse rocked his way forward. He stopped in front of the children and inclined his head graciously.

'Pleased to meet you,' he said in a low and gentle voice. His eyes were large and warm.

'Loyal is our contact above ground,' explained Theo. 'He has been around a long time and is considered very valuable by collectors. He was originally created for a well-to-do Victorian family to help their young son who was afflicted with rickets.'

Milli's face crinkled and Ernest could see she was on the verge of asking what 'crickets' was so he jumped in.

'Rickets was a common disease in Victorian times, caused by inadequate diet and resulting in poor bone development.'

'Exactly right, young Ernest,' said the horse.

'Riding me allowed the young master to develop some strength and mobility in his legs.'

'Who was the boy?' Milli asked.

'Sebastian Von Gobstopper, Gustav's grandfather,' said the rocking horse with an affection that had not diminished with time.

The children instinctively put out their hands to stroke him. His muzzle was smooth and warm and his coat well brushed. He had been carefully preserved and didn't appear to have a scratch on him. His honey eyes twinkled at their touch and the children couldn't help but like him immediately. He reminded them of an old tree — strong, protective and not easily shifted.

'Loyal is to be your transport should you need him,' put in the soldier. 'He can be surprisingly fast when the occasion calls for it.'

'Transport?' echoed Ernest.

'Yes,' said Theo with a very earnest look. 'We have a favour to ask.'

'What is it?' Milli said.

'We need you to venture into the basement. We've never tried as it's too dangerous for us — if we were caught, there wouldn't be much we could do. But you can get in there easily.'

'What if *we're* caught?' Ernest asked.

'You would be seen as two errant children doing some unauthorised exploring — a nuisance but nothing more. The worst-case scenario might be what I believe is called *detention*.'

'We also have something called expulsion,' muttered Ernest glumly.

'Oh, I seriously doubt that would be a consideration — not for St Erudite's star first-former.'

'Theo's right,' said Milli. 'You're far too great an asset to be expelled.'

'I understand the young man's hesitation,' sympathised the bear. 'We would not be asking this if we didn't feel it was a matter of great importance.'

'Our friends are disappearing and we don't know why,' said Pascal.

'If something sinister is going on, we need to expose it,' Captain Pluck added, jumping to his feet and preparing to meet danger head-on. 'We need to know the enemy before we can deal with him!'

'Calm down, Pluck,' advised the wise bear.

'Let us save our energy for when it is really needed.'

'Please help us,' entreated Pascal with a coquettish flutter of her eyelashes.

Ernest sighed. 'It doesn't look like we have much of a choice.'

'Oh, there is always a choice,' mused Theo with a smile. 'It is the choices we make that determine who we are.

'Loyal will come with you,' Theo went on, then added rather cryptically, 'in case he is needed.'

'Won't it be as dangerous for him?' asked Milli.

'Loyal's value gives him immunity,' explained the bear. 'No one would dare harm him.'

And so it was settled. The Resistance toys wished them luck and Loyal led the children out of the underground chamber and up into a part of the arcade they did not recognise from their last visit.

CHAPTER TEN

The Botchers

he three adventurers made their way through the empty gallery, Milli and Ernest holding either side of Loyal's bridle. Milli veered automatically towards the elevator but Loyal shook his head. 'No — too noisy,' was his clipped reply.

As they drew close to where the tour group was standing listening to Fritz, Loyal's ears quivered. The children could see that he was tense. They all slipped behind a wide stone column that managed to completely obscure them. Just ahead they could see and hear the happy commotion as the St Erudite's students wriggled into padded safety suits to take a ride on what Fritz called the Rocket Launch. Milli and Ernest caught the words 'perfectly safe' and 'straight through the atrium roof and back'. It sounded thrilling and they couldn't believe this highlight had been omitted from the first visit. They even felt a little bitter, thinking that they might have flown in the rocket themselves today had they delayed rejoining the toys. But there was no time to gaze regretfully at the group standing around the silver bullet that was starting to spit sparks. Loyal nudged them gently and steered them into a side corridor.

A dusty staircase led downwards into the bowels of the arcade. Across the top, to deter their descent, was a sign reading: *Arcade Staff Only — Trespassers Prosecuted*. They ducked nimbly around the sign, more worried about being seen than what prosecution might entail. Milli wondered how Loyal was going to navigate the stairs, but he balanced his weight on his rockers and used them like skis, sliding down the steps in slow motion.

Ernest began to seriously regret their decision when, halfway down, they came to a small landing where a medical trolley stood, packed with jars. He tried not to look too closely at the jars' murky contents after he glimpsed one holding a collection of giant eyes suspended in a clear jelly. He shuddered, and hoped they were only glass, but they rolled around the jar in order to follow the group's descent. Milli didn't notice, too keen on being first to reach the basement, and Ernest thought it best not to point them out to her.

The stairs ended in a heavy metal door, the kind that, once opened, springs back immediately upon release. Above it was a sign that simply read *Basement Level*. They opened the door and stepped into a long corridor lit by overhead fluorescent lights. It took them some seconds to adjust to the brightness. The floor was flecked grey linoleum and highly polished, and the air smelled of cleaning agents, not dissimilar to how Ernest's house smelled after his mother had gone on one of her cleaning binges. For some unaccountable reason, this sterile corridor was more frightening than if they'd stepped into a dark cave full of bats. It felt like a mausoleum — cold and devoid of life.

They had to tread carefully for they found the linoleum squeaked if they moved too fast. Loyal moved so smoothly and silently that the children concluded his rockers must be felt-lined. Both Milli and Ernest clung on to his reins, more for a sense of security than anything else. All the time they were conscious of the possibility of being discovered and felt extremely exposed walking down the middle of this deserted corridor with nothing in sight that might work to conceal their presence.

The hollow silence made the hairs on Milli's neck prickle. 'Where are we?' she breathed.

Looking at the wide-eyed expression on Loyal's face she could see he was thinking the same. Whatever the rocking horse had imagined finding, it wasn't this. He didn't know what to make of it. His spongy nostrils flared and his breathing quickened.

Ernest, too, was uncomfortable. His fingers holding the reins had gone rigid and he couldn't seem to relax them. Whatever it was that lurked within the basement, Ernest was sure it was something much more sinister than a monster. Monsters, as a rule, could be outsmarted if you were quick-witted and didn't panic. But he wasn't sure he was ready to face whatever was concealed down here.

Other polished corridors branched off the main one, like ancillary roads running off a highway. Occasionally they came to a series of closed doors, most with glass panels. Some appeared to be supply closets, because when the children peered inside they could see containers with labels like *Furry Appendages*, *Assorted Paws* and *Mechanical Limbs*. In one they saw sacks spilling their contents of synthetic hair in different shades. Another supply room looked like a wrecker's yard, with rusty saws, metal prongs and boxes spilling screws all over the floor. At the end of the corridor was a set of double swinging doors with a sign above that said *Quiet Please — Surgery in Progress*. That made them believe they might be in a toy hospital but then other rooms incongruously named *Accessories Lab* and *Objects Blunt and Sharp* completely confused them.

The sound of conversation reached them as they rounded a corner. They followed it to a door with *Botchers' Common Room* written above it.

'What on earth's a Botcher?' Ernest whispered.

Loyal's brow creased and he shook his head to indicate that he could not enlighten them.

Milli and Ernest crept closer, with Loyal watching them, poised to spring at the slightest sign of trouble. They had to stand on their tiptoes to peer into the room and even then their eyes only just reached to where the glass panel began.

Nothing terribly exciting appeared to be going on inside the room, which looked a little like the waiting lounge in an airport where passengers sit counting off the time before boarding their flights. The occupants were mostly men in lab coats, bespectacled and greying. They were sitting in leather armchairs, reading papers or sipping coffee, and by the semi-recumbent positions of some you could tell they had been there for a while. They had a look of being temporarily marooned and nobody was making any move to resume their duties. In one corner was a bar where some people downed amber liquid from tumblers. Two men were engrossed in a game of chess. Another had nodded off in the midst of reading a journal, which had slipped from his hands onto his thighs. A very unhospital-like smell of alcohol and tobacco seeped from the room.

The children were just close enough to overhear the conversation of a pair seated near the door. One had a receding hairline and the other a carefully groomed goatee that he stroked at regular intervals.

'How long before we have to get back to work?' one of the men said.

'At least an hour,' his colleague replied, stretching his legs and glancing at his wristwatch.

'Oh well, can't complain. They should have school groups in more often.' The balding man smiled.

'Makes a welcome change from reconstructive surgery,' added the bearded man and they both chortled with laughter.

'God, this place is depressing,' muttered another man nearby, putting down his newspaper.

'Quit moaning,' the bearded man snapped. 'No one's holding a gun to your head.'

'Let's see what you say if the truth ever comes out,' taunted the other.

The children looked back at Loyal. He rolled his eyes frantically, indicating that they should come away. They crept back towards him and all moved a safe distance from the Botchers' Common Room.

'I think they might be toy doctors,' said Ernest. 'They seem to be waiting for the kids to leave before they can get back to work.'

'What did that doctor mean by "the truth"?' puzzled the rocking horse. 'And what exactly is this work that can't be resumed until the excursion is over? This is strange indeed.'

'Perhaps they can't be distracted by noise when working,' suggested Ernest, even though he knew this was implausible. Whatever noise the children upstairs were making, it seemed unlikely that any of it would filter down as far as the basement.

'Where to now?' said Milli.

'I think that might be enough for one day,' Loyal replied, his voice rumbling with disquiet. 'We need to report back to Theo. He will know what the next step should be.'

Ernest heartily concurred, but Milli wasn't convinced.

'Report back?' she objected. 'There's nothing to report. We need to keep looking, at least for a little while.'

'Very well,' Loyal reluctantly agreed. 'If that is what you think.'

'But only for ten more minutes,' put in Ernest. 'We have to get back to the others. We can't be left behind a second time.'

'But we don't have to get back,' Milli reminded him. 'We're not officially here so we won't be missed. We can make our own way home later.'

There was nothing to direct them through the maze of windowless corridors, so they headed down the nearest one in the hope that it might lead somewhere useful. But it stretched ahead emptily and Milli began to worry that they would have to abort their mission having discovered little of value. They were on the verge of heading back when the sound of banging and crashing drew their attention. There was a door ahead that was ajar and when they peeked inside they saw the messiest workroom they had ever laid eyes upon. It wasn't a clinical room like the others they'd seen; in here were dusty bookcases, antique vases and old wicker furniture. The giant heads of stone gargoyles sat grinning on the floor and there was a statue of some classical deity so large its head touched the ceiling. There was a tea trolley holding plates of half-eaten sandwiches and dainty cakes that had only been nibbled at the edges. Various drawing utensils were strewn across the floor; tattered sheets hung from the overhead fan. There was an easel and numerous brushes in jars. Strange markings and rudimentary sketches even covered the walls, which were decorated with a silver grey wallpaper with a dragonfly imprint. Everywhere the children looked they saw strange objects: giant syringes filled with brightly coloured sizzling liquid, candelabra in the shape of intertwined test tubes, glass specimen domes holding beetles and exotic butterflies the size of bread-and-butter plates. The occasional tables were made from tree trunks with twisted branches for legs. A series of antique bird cages held colourful birds made of papier-mâché. A red velvet chaise lounge held an assortment of rare toys — a sailor bear, three French dolls, and a dragon with shimmering scales.

In the midst of the chaos stood a woman in black, tall and ghoulish. Her eyes were shut and she seemed to be lost in thought. A black cat leapt onto the tea trolley, sniffed indifferently at what it found there, then jumped down to rub itself around its mistress's legs, purring for attention.

'Not now, Socrates!' snapped the woman. 'Can't you see I'm busy.'

The cat continued undeterred and the woman opened her eyes, the mood broken.

'Infuriating animal!' she muttered under her breath and began to hurl whatever small objects she could reach across the room. Socrates scuttled for cover and the children flinched as a coffee cup shattered against a pillar, followed by the pages of a notepad fluttering through the air and a storm of pens that rained down on the floor. Without so much as a glance at the damage she had caused, the woman settled herself comfortably at a large round table that held sheets of butcher's paper and an assortment of crayons. She picked one up and set to work on a rather flamboyant sketch.

Now that she was seated the children were able to get a better look at her. She had long hair the colour of pitch on one side of her head; on the other it had been cropped as short as a pixie's and dyed ox-blood red. There were dark rings under her eyes, as if she were sleep deprived, and her mouth was painted an extraterrestrial silver. Her skin was bluish-white which gave her the appearance of being frozen. She was as lanky as a bean stalk and dressed in a torn black lace dress, so flimsy that part of her skeletal chest was visible. On her feet were boots that came to arrow-sharp points, and she had a black leather jacket with metal studs on the upturned collar over her shoulders. A tattoo of a serpent wound its way up her pale arm.

Suddenly she jerked to her feet as if struck by an idea, and began an animated conversation with someone on the other side of the room. She batted her eyelids, gasped and giggled like a school girl, and patted her chest. The children strained to see who else was in the room but saw nothing but a marble bust propped on an antique barley-twist pedestal.

'I am unworthy of your time, Brilliant One,' the woman said. 'But I will learn. Just be patient, grant me time.'

155

When Milli and Ernest looked at Loyal, his mane was bristling. What was wrong? Milli didn't get a chance to ask because the woman began singing, closing her eyes and resting her cheek alongside the cold marble head. She clearly had difficulty holding a tune — no sooner had she started in one particular key than she jumped to another without showing the least awareness of having done so. What started as a chant grew in momentum and volume until the woman was standing on the table playing air guitar and belting out the words as if she were in front of an audience of thousands.

I've met Coco, Calvin and Gianni,
Luis, Marc and Armani,
They make handbags, blouses and evening
  wear,
But there's one thing they can't do and
  wouldn't dare.

They couldn't design a toy in a blind pink fit,
They'd need manuals, assistants and
  instruction kits.
In all the world there is only one

156

Girl who can really get things done.
That girl is here for all to see,
They'll never know my secrets, I'm a
*   mystery.*

My designs will go down in history!
I'm warped and twisted,
I'll cop some flack.
Most people think I'm a maniac …

Milli's and Ernest's fear left them momentarily.

'Don't think she'll be signing any record deals in a hurry,' Ernest smirked.

'Really?' said Milli in mock surprise. 'I think she'll go far, whoever she is.'

Loyal's face looked both surprised and troubled. 'Are you saying that neither of you recognise that person?' he asked.

Ernest squinted for a closer look and then let out an audible gasp. Milli struggled to comprehend.

'What?' she said.

'That's *her*,' Ernest mouthed in disbelief. 'That's the curator.'

Part III

Dark Discoveries

CHAPTER ELEVEN

Fritz Braun

iscovering the curator in her workshop looking so wild and behaving so erratically convinced even Milli that it was time to beat a hasty retreat. As they backed away from the door and found the stairs that had led them down to the basement, a jumble of questions formed in Milli's mind. It felt as if a ball of wool had got tangled in her head. What had happened to the previously austere curator? Who were the Botchers and what sort of work did they perform? The basement's intricate network of passageways was surely being used for something more sinister than restoration.

For a moment Milli considered whether they should seek assistance from other sources, but immediately dismissed the idea. They had no evidence of wrongdoing, or even negligence for that matter. And even if they had, who would take the matter seriously given that the alleged victims were toys and the suspected perpetrator a woman who liked to dress up in different outfits and talk to statues in her spare time? Eccentricity, after all, wasn't against the law. There really was nothing to be done but continue their investigations alone.

Milli could just imagine Mrs Perriclof's reaction: 'Talking toys! Really, Ernest, that is the absolute limit. I think it might be time for you to broaden your friendship group.' She thought of POSSOM arriving on the scene and searching the doll perambulators for illicit substances. The news would spread that Drabville's child heroes had finally lost the plot, that fame had eroded their sense of reality. Others might accuse them of saying or doing anything for attention. No, Milli decided, this was definitely not the time for adult intervention.

Ernest, meanwhile, was racking his brains for a Shakespearean quote that might come close to describing their situation. He wasn't successful.

The children inched open the heavy metal door at the foot of the stairs as quietly as they could, and found a frowning Fritz Braun standing on the other side, his arms folded across his chest as if he had been expecting them. All traces of his friendly demeanour had vanished. He scowled at them darkly.

'What are you doing down here?' he barked. 'Are you out of your minds? Can you not read signs?'

Milli thought she detected a hint of fear in his voice, not completely masked by his anger. She thought frantically for an acceptable explanation but Fritz's glare unsettled her and she couldn't think properly. Ernest was looking at her imploringly, expecting her to come up with an explanation.

'We … got lost?' she offered weakly.

'Nonsense!' snapped Fritz. 'You don't honestly expect me to believe that.' He leaned in closer to the children and his words took on a greater urgency. 'Now I don't know what you two have been up to, but you're going to leave right away. This is no place for children. Go now and I promise not to tell the curator you were here.'

He took a step towards them and Loyal made a defensive snorting sound. Fritz took in the rocking horse for the first time and his eyes widened in shock.

'Loyal?' he said. 'Can it be you?'

The rocking horse looked confused before giving a guarded answer. 'That is my name.'

'Don't you remember me?' said Fritz, dropping to his knees and now looking as excited as a child. 'I used to play with you when I visited my uncle's country house as a little boy. You remember, in the nursery overlooking the park?'

Loyal scrutinised Fritz closely and the beginnings of a smile creased the corners of his mouth.

'My dear Fritz!' he exclaimed. 'How you have changed. When I saw you last, you were a chubby, round-faced boy. But that must have been at least ten years ago, surely!'

'I wouldn't say I was chubby,' Fritz objected.

164

'But you, on the other hand, have not changed at all.'

'Made to last,' said Loyal. 'It's good to see you again.'

Fritz put his arm around the horse's neck and the children felt they were witnessing the reunion of old friends.

'What happened to you?' continued Loyal, his expression changing from pleasure to consternation. 'You used to visit regularly and then you just stopped coming. I worried about you.'

Fritz's face clouded over and he looked suddenly self-conscious. 'That was my parents' idea,' he said. 'There was a falling-out — it happens in families. They cut contact with my uncle, believing him to be … what were their words … *a damaging influence*. I was sent away to boarding school in Switzerland and spent the next seven years studying Logic and Mathematics, but they gave me little satisfaction. As soon as I was old enough, I ran away and went to work for Von Gob Toys, my uncle's company. He had a factory then in Vienna, and I lived in the rooms upstairs. My parents searched for me but I managed to elude them.'

'Have you seen your uncle recently?' asked Loyal with concern.

'No,' said Fritz. 'He wrote to me about the opening of the arcade and asked me to join him here. But when I arrived he was nowhere to be found. The new managers say he handed over administrative duties to them so that he can retire and resume his life as a recluse, but I think it odd that he would cut off *all* communication.'

'Odd is exactly what it is,' agreed the horse.

'You don't believe it either?'

'Strange things are happening here,' Loyal said. 'Things your uncle would never approve of.'

'You are quite right,' Fritz admitted. He looked as if he might be on the verge of sharing something with them, and then reconsidered. He gave a furtive look down the corridor beyond the open steel door.

'Please tell us what you know,' Milli said encouragingly.

'Can you come back later? We can talk then without being interrupted. There's never anyone down here after six.'

Fritz's pager beeped. He withdrew it and shook his head as he read the text on its screen.

'I have to go now,' he said quickly. 'Our chief designer is calling for fresh coffee. We'll meet back here later.'

'Do you mean the curator?' Ernest called after him, but Fritz was already walking away down the corridor, grumbling about being 'reduced to a manservant', and did not look back.

When Milli got home, she gave her father perfunctory answers to questions about her day and quickly asked whether she could go to Ernest's to help him learn his lines for his part in the upcoming Christmas play. She added that Ernest had invited her to stay for dinner so they needn't set a place for her. Dorkus looked at her sister with suspicion but Mr Klompet raised no objection. He agreed to pick her up when they were done, but insisted that Milli try a piece of his beetroot slice before she left as it was a while till dinner. At the Perriclof home Ernest had spun his parents a similar story and the children met as planned on the corner of Ernest's street,

Bauble Lane, before heading off in the direction of the arcade.

When they returned to the underground headquarters, there was some time to spare before their meeting with Fritz Braun so they filled in the others on what they had encountered in the basement. Then they noticed that Pascal was not present.

'She should be here any minute,' said Theo.

When Pascal did appear some minutes later, her face was tear-stained and she was walking unevenly. It transpired that she had lost a slipper whilst making her way through the labyrinthine tunnels and had been unable to find it.

Captain Pluck raised his eyebrows and folded his arms impatiently. 'Pascal!' he scolded. 'There are more important things than the loss of a shoe.' Theo shook his head in warning but the damage was done.

'More important perhaps for you!' spluttered the now red-faced doll. 'All you want to do is prance around in your uniform feeling important. I would so much rather be upstairs with my friends who understand me.'

'You don't mean that,' said Theo. 'We must stay together until we know what's happening.'

'If we weren't fussing over Pascal all the time, we might actually get more done,' snapped the soldier. 'Useless, conceited doll.'

'I may be useless and conceited,' shrilled Pascal, her accent becoming more pronounced the angrier she became, 'but at least I'm not a joke.'

'Madam, retract that immediately! If I were not a soldier and a gentleman —'

'Enough bickering,' interjected Loyal. 'Perhaps we will be able to shed more light on things after our meeting. In the meantime, let's try to remain calm.'

'He who wavers is lost,' Ernest added sagely. He didn't know whether it was Shakespeare or not but it had the effect of making Theo burst into thunderous laughter. The others soon followed and the tension in the room temporarily lifted.

They met up with Fritz as planned and he led them to his room via the elevator. Milli and Ernest thought the word *cubicle* might be a better way to describe it. The walls and floor were concrete and the iron bed was narrow with a thin foam mattress. There was a small metal trunk by the bed which appeared to contain all of Fritz's worldly possessions. His clothes hung from a portable rack and there was a ceramic wash basin with a jug balanced on it. Milli and Ernest knew from their research that Von Gobstopper had no children and it surprised them that the heir to the toy empire should be living in such reduced circumstances.

'Not exactly what you expected?' Fritz asked, reading their thoughts. The children smiled uncomfortably, not wishing to cause him further embarrassment.

'I would invite you to sit down,' Fritz said with a self-deprecating smile, 'but standing is probably more comfortable.'

Loyal invited the children to climb onto his back in order to free up some space.

'But Von Gobstopper is your uncle,' Milli finally blurted, unable to contain her curiosity any longer. 'And he's worth millions!'

'He is,' said Fritz cheerfully, 'but he does not appear to be here now, does he?' Although he was making light of the situation, his blue eyes were like icebergs. 'Are you always so direct?' he asked Milli.

'Not always but usually,' she said carefully. 'In my experience, it saves an awful lot of mucking about.'

'Where do you think your uncle is?' asked Ernest.

'I have thought about it, and it is my view that he is right here, somewhere in this arcade,' replied Fritz matter-of-factly.

Milli was shocked. 'Doing what exactly?'

'Not *doing* anything in particular but being held prisoner.' Fritz surveyed them carefully and rubbed his chin. 'Before I go on, I feel I should warn you that this is not something you want to involve yourselves in. It would be far better if you left this place and resumed your normal lives. The longer you spend here, the more danger you put yourselves in.'

'We can't leave now,' Milli protested. 'Not without knowing that Theo, Pascal and Captain Pluck are safe!'

'You're quite a determined girl, aren't you?' Fritz said. 'How old are you both?'

171

'Just turned thirteen. We were born a month apart,' said Milli and then for the first time in her life, she found herself wishing she were older, just so she might make more of an impression on this worldly boy. She was most put out when Fritz made a whistling sound through his teeth.

'Just babies,' he muttered.

'We're extraordinarily mature for our age,' Milli contradicted huffily.

'Thirteen marks the onset of adolescence,' added Ernest, 'and the end of childhood. So babies, I think, is hardly an appropriate word.'

'I apologise if I have offended,' said Fritz with a humble bow. 'You have achieved a good deal for your young years. If you wish to stay and help, I would be honoured.'

'This morning we caught a glimpse of Ms Anomali talking to a marble bust,' said Milli.

'Ms Anomali is a designer — what did you expect?'

'What does she design?'

'Why, toys, of course. She has taken on the position of chief designer for Von Gob Toys. She wants to revolutionise the company, make cheaper toys and appeal to the mass market. She claims that my uncle has given her free rein.'

'But Von Gob Toys have always been unique, never two the same in the entire world,' said Ernest.

'Yes, that was the case,' said Fritz, 'but I fear it is about to change now that my uncle has *retired*.'

'And what's all this business going on in the basement?' interposed Loyal.

'It is not a basement, old friend,' Fritz said slowly. 'It's a laboratory.'

Fritz's words hung heavily in the air. Nobody spoke for a long moment and then Loyal found his voice.

'A laboratory for what?'

'Modifications,' murmured Fritz. 'That is the job of the Botchers. They are plastic surgeons whose licences have been revoked so they can no longer practise in the human world.'

'Why are they here?' asked Loyal in an ominous voice.

'It is not something that can be easily explained,' floundered Fritz. 'I would have to

173

show you. I think it is time for a visit to Hack Ward. Perhaps, together, we can work out what's going on.'

Fritz's words seemed to release a valve in Ernest's brain, which he felt was on the verge of imploding. He was, admittedly, also irritable and hungry as he'd not had time for an afternoon snack.

'No, we're not sure we can handle it!' he shouted. 'Why should we be expected to? We've been through enough drama in the last year to last most people a lifetime and yet here we are again, facing danger and uncertainty and not an adult in sight to soften the blow. I know what Milli and I should be doing right now. We should be at home doing our homework or watching an episode of *So You Think You're a Genius* on the telly' — Milli raised her eyebrows dubiously at this — 'before brushing our teeth and taking a mug of warm milk to bed. That's what kids our age should be doing, not worrying about kidnapped toymakers and insane designers. There are debating tryouts at school tomorrow and we're going to be too wrung out to do our best because we're too busy trying to catch —' He stopped suddenly, conscious of having held the floor uninterrupted for the duration of this outburst. He took a deep breath and regained his composure. 'Of course we can handle it,' he said, and looked at Milli for confirmation.

Milli looked at Ernest as if she was seeing him for the first time. 'Lead the way,' she said, even though her heart was pounding in her chest.

CHAPTER TWELVE

Hack Ward

Fritz led the way to a stark corridor where the floors were pale grey and plastic chairs in a salmon pink colour were arranged in a row against the walls. The identical doors that lined the corridor were painted a maroon colour that reminded them of congealed blood. Fritz stopped abruptly in front of one of the doors.

'This is Hack Ward,' he announced. 'This is a high-security area — where toys come for rehabilitation, so we're told.'

'What are we waiting for?' Loyal asked, going to push the door open with his nose.

Fritz stepped in front of him and barred the

way. He looked particularly at the children and his tone turned sombre.

'Before you go in, I think you should be prepared. I don't know exactly what goes on in here, but the sight that greets you behind this door may be confronting. I'm afraid your memories of childhood may be altered permanently.'

The children nodded to indicate that they understood and were prepared to accept any ramifications. Fritz hesitated a moment longer then slowly turned the handle and pushed open the door.

At first glance the room looked like a regular hospital ward. There were rows of metal beds, monitors, drips, and clipboards with the patient's history hanging from bed ends. The lights had been dimmed and the room was tinged with blue, giving it a surreal quality. The children wondered whether this was for the patients' comfort. On a trolley by the door lay an assortment of implements, not all of them surgical in nature: scalpels, a variety of hooks, scissors, an enormous metal file, sponges in basins, a staple gun, a drill and a collection of knives. A drawer in one of the bedside cabinets

177

had been left half open and inside they could see tubes of adhesive and a blowtorch.

The curtains, also a washed-out blue, around the beds were open so the patients were clearly visible. As it has been established that this was some kind of toy hospital, many of you may now be hoping for a charming scene of teddies in plaster recovering from broken legs or dolls in slings or a golly with an icepack over its eye to reduce the swelling sustained from falling from a display or even a minor scuffle. If so, you should perhaps consider jumping to the next chapter, or even the last page of this book, to spare yourself unnecessary upset. I would like to spare you that upset myself, but in the interest of truth I cannot. For the truth is that life is not always (or even often) a bed of roses. It is full of pleasures and delights, yes, but unpleasant things also happen and often to those with the least means of defending themselves. I am of the opinion that it would be unwise for us as children to shy away from these things altogether. If we do, we run the risk of being caught unawares, and when we are caught unawares there is not much we can do to prevent such things from happening again. So, if you are still with me, steel yourself and let us continue.

Although Milli and Ernest, as we know, had seen many extraordinary things in their young lives, nothing they had previously encountered prepared them for the grisly sights that greeted them in Hack Ward. Images of what they saw that day would stay with them for years to come, popping unexpectedly into their heads and jarring them from whatever pleasant activity they happened to be engaged in at the time. Could they have predicted such repercussions they might have reconsidered their decision, but I seriously doubt it.

On the little beds in neat rows lay an assortment of toys in various stages of convalescence. It was the toys' appearance that made Ernest recoil and Milli's jaw drop. Both children, resilient as they were, found themselves frozen in horror. Loyal's reaction, perhaps buffeted by experience, was merely to look immeasurably sad.

On the bed nearest to them lay what had once been a doll. But surgery, if such it can be called, had altered her to the extent that she barely passed as a doll any longer. Her face had been cut open from chin to eyebrows leaving a gaping slash from which sprang tiny dinosaurs with razor-sharp teeth and claws. One side of the doll's head had been shaved and the blonde hair that remained was matted. An opening in her plastic abdomen showed a screwdriver protruding like a third arm. Her feet had been replaced by feline paws.

All around were toys in a similar condition. In the next bed, a doll had drill screws in place of fingernails. In another, a wide-eyed fleecy bear had the rippling torso of an action hero and carried miniature saws in both paws. A Mr Plod toy had had most of his body removed and replaced with jumbled chess pieces interwoven with shards of metal and glass. Grotesquely, his face was still bright-eyed and smiling. There was a two-headed doll with vampire fangs and barbed-wire hair, and a fairy doll with a rusty spear welded to her arm in place of a wand. In a corner, a tin soldier swung from a crane-like apparatus; a small sign above him read *Awaiting Treatment*.

The toys in Hack Ward had been snipped and stitched and twisted and chopped and put together again in the wrong order. It was a monstrous mutation of objects originally created to generate feelings of warmth and belonging. Surrounding the beds were monitors as well as a tangle of cords, wires and transparent bags containing bright fluids connected to a part of the patients' bodies. The toys all wore identification tags fastened around their wrists. The fact that the patients were toys and obviously not breathing did not lessen the gruesomeness of what had been done to them.

One of the dolls' eyelids fluttered briefly and it sent a monitor into a frenzy. In response purple fluid spurted through one of the tubes. The doll jerked and was immediately motionless again. It was also impossible not to notice that every toy had some kind of weaponry grafted onto its anatomy.

Milli, Ernest and Loyal avoided eye contact with each other, for fear of seeing their own reaction mirrored in the other's gaze. Milli's limbs felt leaden and she had to focus hard to will them to move. The terrible sight of these poor toys meant only one thing to her. Even though she dared not say it out loud, it looked like the work of Lord Aldor the Illustrious. But he had been dismembered back in Mirth. Milli herself had seen him carried off in a cart by the slavish Federico Lampo. It wasn't possible that he could have returned so soon. Even a magician of his calibre needed time to regroup. But when she looked at Ernest's face she knew he was thinking very similar thoughts. The toys in Hack Ward weren't the result of random vandalism by curious children who had pulled the arms off their dolls or the stuffing out of their teddies to see how they were made. The mutations they saw in Hack Ward clearly had some kind of *purpose.*

Milli looked up and realised that Fritz was watching her with concern. She had been biting hard on her lower lip to stay calm but when he patted her shoulder awkwardly, she buried her face in his shirt to hide her tears. The group stood in silence, searching for something appropriate to say. Finally, Loyal spoke.

'Something is very wrong here, but remember, toys have been the allies of children for centuries.

It would take something more extraordinary than an operation to change that ... Let's get out of here,' he said quietly.

'We can't just leave them,' Milli said, reaching a hand out towards the nearest toy.

'Touch nothing,' said Fritz firmly. 'They mustn't know we've been here.'

Loyal nodded firmly in agreement. 'Fritz is right. Giving ourselves away now will help no one.'

Seeing Milli's distressed face, Fritz added, 'We'll come back — I promise.'

Ernest was just reaching for the door when they heard the tapping sound of sharp heels on a polished floor. Tempest Anomali was coming in their direction and she wasn't alone. They could hear her speaking to someone in a berating tone. They had barely enough time to huddle together on one of the empty beds and draw the curtains around them before the door was flung open so violently its metal handle smashed into the wall.

'Dr Savage, so far you have made me only empty promises!' Tempest screeched. 'The board wants to see results!'

The group could see her feet beneath the curtain as she marched through the ward like a commandant inspecting troops. What she saw clearly did not impress her.

'Not good enough!' she yelled and stamped her feet.

Her companion tried to mollify her. 'We are moving as quickly as we can,' he said. 'These things take time to fine-tune. It's a relatively new field of endeavour —'

'I am not after the Nobel Prize, Savage. *Fine-tuning*, as you put it, is not high on my list of priorities. Sometimes I wonder whether you are deserving of being called a Botcher.'

'Perhaps if we had access to the secret manual,' the man suggested.

'Yes, that would be *useful*,' Tempest said between gritted teeth. They could imagine the look of fury crossing her face. 'Unfortunately, and as you well know, we have not yet been able to procure it.'

'But surely the toymaker could be persuaded to —'

'He is proving more stubborn than we expected for an old git, but there is another tactic I'm about to try and I don't expect to fail.'

'I'm sure you will succeed,' fawned the man.

Tempest's rage abated a little with the flattery.

'I'll be generous and give you another week to produce something impressive,' she said.

'Don't be fooled by appearances. The specimens you see before you may look comical but are more vicious than you would believe,' said the Botcher, but it was a poor strategy as it served only to infuriate Tempest again.

'Don't insult my intelligence, Savage,' she snapped. 'This looks like the rubbish you'd find in a flea market! Try at least to understand the essence of my drawings and stop taking so many short cuts. After all, short cuts are what landed you here in the first place.'

'We'll do our best,' the doctor replied, sounding as if he was struggling to maintain his composure.

'You'd better. Otherwise, it's back to unemployment and you know what that means?' Tempest snarled. 'No more Club Med holidays or the best grammar school for the kiddies.'

With that final barb, she pushed past the stunned doctor and flounced out through the door. Dr Savage performed a hasty round of the ward and tweaked a few tubes, before slinking out himself, like a dog with its tail between its legs.

The main concern preoccupying the group now was the welfare of the toymaker. Fritz's theory had been correct: Von Gobstopper was being held somewhere in the arcade. Finding him became a matter of urgency.

'What's this secret manual they mentioned?' Ernest asked. Fritz frowned.

'I think I might have an idea, although I can't be sure as it happened so long ago. I was very young at the time but I distinctly remember Uncle Gustav telling me about having inherited a friend's private notebook. He was worried about it falling into the wrong hands.'

'Why, what was in it?' Milli asked.

'He didn't say exactly, just that it contained valuable information, information that could prove dangerous.' Milli and Ernest exchanged glances. The mention of wrong hands had triggered disturbing memories.

'There's someone we suspect could be involved; someone we've had dealings with before,' Milli said hesitantly.

'He's known as Lord Aldor,' continued Ernest.

'Who is this person?' Fritz demanded.

'Just the sort of person who would be interested in information that could be used to further his own ends, the sort of individual you wouldn't want to know if you could help it.'

'We'll tell you more about him later,' said Milli.

'Do you think your uncle still has the notebook?' Ernest asked.

'I'm certain of it. We must find him. He has to be in the building somewhere.'

'We'll search every floor!' exclaimed the rocking horse.

'It would help if we knew where to start,' said Fritz.

As if in answer, several loud beeps sounded, making them all jump in alarm. It was the doctor's pager, which he'd inadvertently left behind on one of the beds. There was no time to lose. Dr Savage would soon realise his oversight and return to collect it. Milli pocketed the pager before anyone could even offer an opinion and headed out the door to find Theo and the others.

'Quick thinking,' said Fritz admiringly, once they had regained the safety of the stairwell.

'As long as it doesn't raise any suspicion,' qualified the ever-cautious Ernest.

'Better read the message,' urged Loyal, 'before we decide whether it will be of any use or not.'

'All right,' said Milli, withdrawing the shiny gadget from her blazer pocket. They all crowded around her to read the message flashing on the black screen. The message on Dr Savage's pager provided them with a vital piece of information. 'Collect old man from monument and bring him to me at 8 sharp.'

Milli and Ernest smiled. Luck, it seemed, was finally on their side. There was only one minor problem: they didn't remember seeing any monuments, large or small, in the parts of the arcade they had been through.

Fritz was only too aware that his uncle's safety now depended largely on him. 'The monument … where could that be?' he said anxiously. He frowned, willing himself to remember. When nothing came to him he grew agitated and began pacing and pressing his palms to his forehead. 'I know I've heard of it before … but I can't think!'

The others could only wait and try to help prod his memory.

'Could it be a special room in the arcade?' asked Milli.

'Monuments can sometimes be tombs,' Ernest suggested.

'No one is buried here that I know of.'

'Is it even in the arcade?' puzzled Loyal.

Fritz stopped pacing and gave Loyal a look of grateful acknowledgment.

'I think I know where it is!' he said. 'And no, it isn't in the building — it's right outside. The monument is the giant statue of my uncle at the entrance.' Congratulatory smiles were exchanged all round.

'Now we know where,' said Ernest, thinking aloud, 'but how does it help us?'

'Doctor Savage is heading there tonight,' Milli reminded them.

'We have to make sure we get there first,' said Fritz.

CHAPTER THIRTEEN

Geppetto's Notebook

fter hours, the arcade had a totally different atmosphere. The group — now joined by the other members of the Resistance — walked through it as though in a tomb. A few of the gaslights had been left on casting dancing shadows on the stone. Security grilles were pulled down over the shops' windows. The only sound was the sharp tapping of their footsteps on the tiled floor, until they were interrupted by rhythmic marching and the beating of toy drums. They retreated behind some decorative carts and watched as a small procession of baton-wielding golliwogs appeared. The golliwogs threw their shoulders back, swelled their chests and lifted their knees ridiculously high as they marched. They wore khaki uniforms and military caps with badges. The leader of the procession was tank-like and had a thuggish expression. Milli knew at once that these weren't original Von Gob toys — their glinting eyes and scowling mouths cut from brilliant red felt told her so. These golliwogs had been altered somehow to become a menacing regiment.

Up until now, the children had only heard about a 'round-up'; now they saw the Golly Police executing one. Moving methodically, the gollies unlocked doors and cabinets and randomly withdrew toys, which they then threw unceremoniously into a laundry cart as if they were nothing more than soiled towels. The toys' limbs jutted out at uncomfortable angles as they were piled on top of one another. Then the drum beat started up again and the patrol moved off around a corner.

'Who were they?' the children asked, horrified by the gollies' callous treatment of their fellow toys.

'The Golly Police,' Fritz said. 'Bred to patrol, a service which, I'm told, gains them certain privileges.'

'Traitors!' whispered Loyal angrily, but Fritz gave a dismissive shrug.

'I suspect corruption has been beyond their control,' he said.

Outside, the children and their toy friends studied the giant stone replica of Gustav Von Gobstopper. They circled, kicked and prodded the immovable stone. It divulged no answers.

'Could there be a password?' agonised Fritz.

No one replied; they all felt as if they had reached an impasse. Their plan to find the toymaker before the doctor did and take him to the safety of the toys' secret headquarters was about to be foiled. What could they do now? In half an hour or so, Dr Savage would come for Von Gobstopper and deliver him to Tempest Anomali. There was no way they could prevent this without access to wherever it was Von Gobstopper was being held.

They decided to position themselves strategically behind some shrubbery and wait.

They figured that once the doctor arrived, a plan might present itself.

They didn't have to wait long. Dr Savage appeared wearing a crumpled suit. He walked purposefully to the colossal statue of the toymaker, stopped in front of it and pulled himself, with some exertion, up onto its base. He rummaged for something in his pockets, and cursed under his breath when he did not immediately find it. Then, from his breast pocket, he withdrew something very small that Ernest thought might be an allen key. They watched him fit it smoothly between a gap in the statue's stone fingers. After some seconds there was a sound like a roll of thunder and the seated statue began to vibrate and then rotated on its base until it was facing the opposite direction. Dr Savage stepped into the exposed opening and disappeared.

Who would have thought that the toymaker was being held prisoner beneath the very statue that celebrated his genius? Wild possibilities raced through the children's minds. Perhaps, once Von Gobstopper emerged, they could distract the doctor and make a run for it. Perhaps together they would be strong enough to tackle him to the ground whilst Pascal guided Von Gobstopper to safety? Whatever they did, they would be giving themselves away and an extensive search for them would surely follow.

Whilst they ruminated on these possibilities, something totally unexpected happened. Without so much as a warning, Captain Pluck charged towards the monument with his rifle cocked. Upon reaching the opening, he let off a round of shots, which still managed to create a loud cracking sound even though it was only a toy weapon.

'Up here, good doctor!' Pluck shouted, despite gesticulations from his companions urging him to turn back.

Dr Savage's face emerged from the hole looking stunned. He looked around for the speaker, then spotted the wooden soldier.

'Come and get me, you bumbling coward,' jeered Captain Pluck.

It took the doctor several moments to get his bearings and realise who was speaking to him. Captain Pluck had been constructed from forty separate pieces of shellacked and painted timber, but was remarkably nimble as he darted between the rose bushes. The doctor stumbled clumsily after the retreating figure of the toy soldier wearing an inspired expression as though he had just made the discovery of the century.

Theo reassured the others that Captain Pluck could take care of himself. The doctor, on the other hand, would be out of breath from pursuing him in just a few minutes. The group descended a steep staircase into a crypt-like room, where they found a fragile old man sitting in a rocking chair with his hands and feet bound. Milli and Ernest recognised him instantly — this was a face that had become familiar all around the globe.

'Uncle!' Fritz cried out, distressed to see the toymaker in such a state. He took Von Gobstopper's papery hand and peered at him.

The sound of his nephew's voice seemed to stir Von Gobstopper out of his stupor. 'Fritz?' he asked. His voice was like sandpaper, scratchy from lack of use. 'What are you doing here? How did you find me?'

'I've been here all the time,' answered Fritz. 'I just didn't know where you were. I'm sorry I couldn't come for you sooner.'

'How could you have known? They did a good job hiding me.'

Loyal coughed and Fritz nodded as he caught the rocking horse's eye. There would be time for explanations later, when they had reached the safety of the Resistance's underground headquarters.

Ernest and Theo supported Von Gobstopper's frail frame like a puppet as Fritz untied his bonds. They all made for the stairs. The toymaker, although dazed, realised their intentions and allowed himself to be directed. He looked as if he'd woken from a prolonged sleep.

When they reached the hideaway, Fritz settled his uncle into a chair. Milli and Earnest were now able to study the toymaker properly. Gustav Von Gobstopper had attained a Rastafarian look from months of neglect. He certainly looked different from the publicity portraits they had seen of him. His face was unshaven and his thin hair unkempt. His body looked as small and shrunken as a balloon after a party. His shoulders sagged and there were dark circles under his eyes. His corduroy trousers were dusty and the green vest patterned with woolly bunnies was frayed at the edges. But despite the overwhelming sense of weariness he conveyed, his blue eyes still held a sparkle.

'Are you all right?' Fritz asked. 'Did they mistreat you?'

'I am fine, just a little stiff, that's all. I was foolish, my boy, allowing myself to be duped like this.'

'Are you aware, Uncle, that terrible things are happening in the arcade?' Fritz said gently, not wishing to alarm the toymaker but not wanting to conceal the truth from him either.

'Hush, Fritz,' Von Gobstopper said. 'I know what is going on in my arcade. Who have you brought with you?' He took off his dusty spectacles and rubbed them on his trouser leg before putting them back on. 'Loyal!' he exclaimed in gleeful recognition. 'And the valiant Theo! You here too, my little Pascal — but how unhappy you look. It is so comforting to see you all again. Come closer and let me see that you are unharmed.'

In the reunion that followed, the toys behaved much like children and Von Gobstopper like a doting parent. It made Milli and Ernest think of their own parents and how worried they must be by now. They also felt a surge of guilt for having lied, even if their intentions had been good.

'And I see you have found friends to lend a hand,' the toymaker said, turning his attention to the children.

'I could not have done it without them,' acknowledged Fritz. 'Uncle, meet Milli Klompet and Ernest Perriclof.'

'Ah,' Von Gobstopper smiled in recognition. 'I know those names. These are the two that led the other children to safety. I have heard much about you both. I extend my thanks to you, Milli and Ernest,' the toymaker said, shaking their hands with a formal solemnity.

Although Von Gobstopper had just escaped real danger, he didn't seem particularly flustered by it, Ernest thought.

'I can see that you are all wondering what is going on,' the old man said. 'It is a long story but I am happy to tell you the abridged version, should you be willing to hear it.'

Everyone nodded, curious to hear what he had to say.

'Well,' he gave a heavy sigh, 'it all began a long time ago in a small village where an accomplished carpenter carved a puppet from a block of pine. The man's name was Geppetto and his loneliness was great. His dearest wish was for a boy to call his own, and his wish was unexpectedly granted by a Blue Fairy, who gave the puppet life and assigned a cricket to act as the puppet's guardian and conscience. The puppet was named Pinocchio and Geppetto loved him as if he were his own flesh and blood. But Pinocchio was constantly being lured into trouble and caused Geppetto only strife. All the boy wanted was to prove his worth, and he was finally able to do so one day when he rescued his creator from the belly of a monstrous whale. It was only then that the Blue Fairy turned Pinocchio into a real boy.'

'It's a beautiful story,' Milli said. 'But what does it have to do with the arcade?'

'Ah,' said Von Gobstopper, 'I have something my kidnappers desperately want. Geppetto kept a notebook in which he recorded all of his inventions, as well as the spell to summon the Blue Fairy. Her power to bring toys to life would prove invaluable to our enemy. They only keep me here in the hope that I will reveal its whereabouts.'

'Do you know the spell to summon the Blue Fairy?' Milli breathed.

Von Gobstopper smiled. 'I do.'

'And the notebook?' Ernest asked.

'That will never be found,' Von Gobstopper said decisively.

'But, Mr Von Gobstopper, they won't stop until they do find it,' warned Ernest.

'They can try as much as they like, but the book no longer exists. I decided to burn it after reading its contents.'

'Why did you do that, Uncle?' asked Fritz. 'Isn't the knowledge it contained now lost forever?'

'Ah,' mused Von Gobstopper, 'I am of the opinion, dear boy, that too much knowledge can be a dangerous thing. But do not fear — the knowledge is safely stored in this old brain. When the time is right it will be passed on to you, Fritz, for safe keeping.'

CHAPTER FOURTEEN

A Visitor in the Night

Even though Milli and Ernest were shivering when they helped each other clamber back through Ernest's bedroom window, they had something more important than the cold on their minds — the time. It was so late, they knew they were unlikely to escape without some serious questioning by their parents. What they weren't expecting was to find both their mothers lying in wait for them.

Mrs Perriclof leapt out of her chair, bundled Ernest into a dressing gown and felt his forehead, but Mrs Klompet stared at her daughter with her arms folded. There was relief in her face but not enough to obliterate the disappointment.

When she spoke her words came out slightly wooden, the way they sometimes do when parents have had too much time to think about what they want to say. She sounded as though she was reading out the instructions on the back of a cake mix packet.

'Milli, I regret to inform you that you are grounded until further notice. You will be escorted to and from school each day as you are clearly not ready for independence. You are both incredibly selfish children to make your parents worry about you like this. Now, get into the car. Your father and Dorkus must be frantic by now.'

'We have a very good reason —' began Milli.

'I don't wish to hear explanations,' interrupted her mother, raising her hand the way a traffic officer might.

'How could you be so thoughtless?' added Ernest's mother. 'Going out in the middle of winter so flimsily dressed. I'm going downstairs immediately to get you both a spoonful of my Fortifying Fish-Tail Tonic.'

'I think the occasion calls for a ladleful,' said a stern-faced Mrs Klompet.

* * *

Milli could hardly bear the tedium of the next few days. She marvelled at Ernest's ability to focus on his lessons when she could do nothing but relive their experiences in the arcade over and over in her mind. Everything else happening around her was a blur. She barely noticed when Mr Sparks set alight a manila folder full of their lab reports whilst attempting to demonstrate the use of a Bunsen burner. She didn't jump back with the others when Articulus Barnes, their elocution master, spat on them during a speech designed to display the power of rhetoric. Nor did she did register why everyone cheered in PE when Gummy Grumbleguts managed to complete the obstacle course without falling into his usual hyperventilating heap. The accumulation of knowledge seemed pointless when the lives of her friends were at stake. What did it matter what the latitudinal position of Trinidad was, or how to calculate the square root of X, if Von Gob Toys died out? On the other hand, Milli knew that she must go about her daily life as normal or risk exposing everything and putting the toys in even graver danger. For once she would have to be patient.

Things were strained at home and it troubled her that a note of suspicion had crept into her parents' conversations with her. Milli didn't want to lose their trust, and hoped that once the truth was known she would be forgiven.

At dinner that evening, Milli pushed her Potato and Pumpkin Mash around her plate and made little peaks in it with her fork. Rosie laid down her knife and fork and looked inquiringly at her daughter.

'Not hungry?'

'No, it's great,' said Milli, shovelling a large forkful into her mouth. The food seemed to stick in her throat and she had to swallow a gulp of Beetroot Cider to wash it down. Crispy Cod Bake with Potato and Pumpkin Mash was normally one of her favourite meals, but tonight she couldn't enjoy it. The food tasted like glue.

Nonna Luna, who was having dinner with the Klompets, looked at Milli with concern. 'Whatta da matta?' she asked. 'You tella Nonna. Nonna fixa for you.'

'It's nothing, Nonna,' Milli mumbled. 'I've just got a lot on at school.'

'Well, it's not going to get any easier,' Dorkus put in unhelpfully. 'The older you get the harder it becomes.'

'As if you'd know,' Milli replied, a little too spitefully.

'Milli's too young to be fretting so much about school work and grades,' said Mr Klompet. 'She still needs to have fun. Never mind about studies — there're years ahead to think of all that.'

'Milli does nothing but have fun!' protested Rosie. 'She's in first year of senior school now and it's time to knuckle down. As Miss Linear never fails to observe, the study habits formed this year are the ones that will stand you in good stead in years to come. Milli has the potential to pursue whatever career she chooses if she applies herself now.'

'She's thirteen, darling heart,' said Mr Klompet, winking at his daughter.

'My point exactly,' said Milli's mother. 'Very soon she'll be an adult. 'It's time she assumed some responsibility.'

'What would you know about responsibility?' Milli snapped. 'All of you are useless! This is the only town in the world that could let a hundred children be kidnapped all at once.'

'Stoppa!' Nonna Luna cut in. 'Milli, no speaka like dat to your mama.'

Rosie looked hurt but Milli couldn't bring herself to apologise. Why couldn't the adults of this town do some of the hard work for once? Why was it always up to the children to save the day? Still, Milli knew in her heart how unfair her criticisms were. After all, it had been her own mother who had expressed caution about the circus until she'd been worn down by the children's persistence.

The meal continued in uncomfortable silence. Milli couldn't even bring herself to be civil to Nonna Luna, whose company she usually delighted in. Nonna looked very downcast when Milli declined a slice of her homemade *tiramisu*, but Milli was too distracted to notice. She went to bed early and, despite the warmth of several patterned quilts, couldn't warm up. The cold filtered like unseen fingers under the door and around the windows where the putty had come loose. Milli found herself lying awake, gazing at the shapes the light from a full moon cast on her ceiling. Her body was tired but her mind simply wouldn't switch off.

The glow of her star-shaped night-light (a present for her third birthday) didn't provide its usual comfort. Milli hadn't slept with the night-light on for some time, but had started using it again since meeting the toys. Images of Hack Ward, kept at bay during the day, always surfaced at this time. Not that the night-light was much help. If it was the dark she was trying to avoid, it'd be fine, but it was her own imagination that was the problem. Right now Milli was imagining the wardrobe door being pushed open by the creature that lurked inside, as well as faces appearing at the window. She gave up and stuck her head under the pillow to escape the show.

When Milli finally did doze off, she felt as if she'd been asleep no more than five minutes before a sound woke her. At first she thought it was the remnant of a dream and ignored it, but it continued. If she wasn't mistaken there was something tapping at the window. The tapping stopped and Milli turned over; then it resumed

— *tap, tap, tap* against the glass. Milli sat bolt upright and stared at the window. There was no one there, only her own image reflected back at her. She remembered what Lucy Carver from school had told her about witches and other dark creatures being attracted by the glow of night-lights and shivered. It was then she heard the voice.

'Let me in,' it begged. 'It's freezing out here!'

Milli scrambled out of bed and pressed her nose against the glass. There outside, falling snow already forming a white mantle on his shoulders, was Loyal the rocking horse. She flung the window open and helped him inside. He was shivering from cold so she threw a rug over him, and rubbed his caramel head while she waited for his teeth to stop chattering.

'How did you get here?' she asked him.

'On my rockers, of course. But I took a few wrong turns. Your little town may be charming but it is very badly signposted!'

'But why are you here? Has something happened?'

'I am afraid I do have bad news,' Loyal puffed. 'Theo sent me as soon as he found out.'

'Found out what?'

Loyal started to answer but broke off suddenly, his ears pricking up. 'Shhh! Someone's coming!'

Sure enough, within seconds the handle of the bedroom door turned and Rosie poked her head into Milli's room. She had gone to bed a little rattled by her daughter's mood at dinner and wanted to check on her. Loyal had just enough time to swing himself into a corner and stand stock-still, which was hard as he had a sudden urge to sneeze.

'Is everything all right?' Rosie asked. 'I thought I heard noises.'

'Just me walking around because I can't sleep,' Milli said, happy not to have to rely on another lie.

'Would a Face Trace help, do you think?' suggested Rosie thoughtfully.

Milli sensed in her mother a desire to make peace and couldn't reject the offer.

'It might,' she said. 'I'm feeling sleepier now.'

Her mother smiled and moved closer to the bed. 'I'm sorry we argued before,' she said. 'I know I'm not always patient and my expectations are sometimes unrealistic. It's just that this family doesn't need any more adventures just now. Agreed?'

'Agreed,' said Milli, feigning a yawn.

Rosie sat on the edge of the bed and stroked the top of Milli's head.

'Now, ready for that Face Trace?'

Milli nodded.

'Okay, then, eyes closed.'

A Face Trace (for those who have never experienced one) was Milli's favourite thing as a child when she couldn't drift off to sleep. It involved her mother tracing the outline of the features on her face with a fingertip and listing each of them each in turn, 'Eyebrows, eyelids, eyelashes …', and it was so soothing that sleep usually came quickly.

'Goodnight, then,' said Rosie, once she had finished.

'Night, Mum, and thanks,' said Milli.

Rosie was just leaving when she spotted the rocking horse. 'Where did that come from?' she said in surprise. 'I've never seen it before.'

'Prop for school play,' mumbled Milli. 'Got him from an op shop. Ernest's idea.'

Rosie seemed satisfied with this and gently closed the door behind her. As soon as she'd gone, Milli sat up. She saw that Loyal was glaring at her.

'I may be old, but I am certainly not op shop material,' he said huffily.

'Keep your voice down,' Milli hissed. 'It was all I could think of. Now please tell me what's going on.'

Loyal's face clouded over and his eyes went misty. 'It's Pascal,' he said with a lump in his throat. 'She's gone missing.'

'Are you sure?' asked Milli, feeling her stomach tighten. 'She sometimes goes off on her own to mope, doesn't she?'

'No, she's really gone this time,' Loyal answered. 'She's been particularly down of late and spoke of rejoining her friends in the arcade. We suspect that's what she's done. Perhaps it wasn't a good idea to impose the ideals of the Resistance on her when she wasn't ready, but now she may have put herself in real danger.'

'What do we do?' Milli asked. Even if Pascal was naïve and foolish, Milli couldn't bear the idea of her falling into the hands of the Botchers. The very thought made her dizzy with fear.

'There is only one thing to do,' replied Loyal. 'We must find Pascal before they do. Put something warm on and climb on my back.'

Milli had just enough time to pull on her sheepskin boots and a fleecy dressing gown before hopping on Loyal's smooth back. Loyal navigated his way around the camellias in the front garden and onto the icy street. He moved lightly and carried Milli's weight with surprising ease. After a few simple directions they turned into Bauble Lane.

Ernest, who was a deep sleeper, proved more difficult to rouse and only when Milli's tapping on his window turned to thumping did he wake with a jolt and tumble onto the floor. Even after he'd opened his window, invited them in and wrapped himself in his dressing gown, he was still rubbing sleep from his eyes.

'Who's gone where?' he mumbled.

'We have to go *now*,' Milli emphasised. 'I'll explain on the way.'

It was an exhilarating ride, zigzagging their way through cobbled streets on Loyal's sturdy back, the night air stinging their cheeks. The rocking horse used the children's weight to propel himself forward and skied along swiftly on his polished rockers. The wind freed Milli's hair from its ribbons so that it streamed behind her. Ernest, fearing they would run into a hedge or picket fence at any moment, kept his head buried in Milli's back.

'Ernest, look!' Milli said, poking his ribs so he had to open his eyes. There was the night sky sprinkled with stars and the soft snow starting to swirl like a shawl around them. Even Ernest had to admit it was quite a sight.

Captain Pluck, Theo and Von Gobstopper were waiting for them in the underground headquarters. Captain Pluck, who had never had much sympathy for Pascal, was having difficulty curbing his criticism.

'Foolish doll!' he burst out when the children arrived. 'Flighty, air-headed twit! Should have known she'd jeopardise everything.'

'That isn't going to help,' Theo reminded him. 'Besides, Pascal hasn't jeopardised anything. She simply made a choice to leave.' Although his voice was level and calm, his muddy brown eyes gave him away — they couldn't mask his distress over their missing compatriot. 'Pascal may have done a stupid thing but she is one of us and we have to help her.'

'I don't know what we can do,' objected Captain Pluck, 'without putting us all at risk. Strategically, it doesn't make sense.'

Their argument was cut short by Fritz's arrival. His face was pinched as he greeted the children.

'It's too late,' he said. 'I've been up to the arcade and looked everywhere. Pascal's not there. She must have been taken during the last round-up.'

A gloomy silence followed. Then Von Gobstopper jumped resolutely to his feet.

'Too many of my creations have disappeared into that basement never to return,' he said. 'I'm not going to let that happen to Pascal. I'm going to find her.'

'Uncle, calm down,' pleaded Fritz, taking him gently by the arm. 'You're not strong enough yet. You stay here with Pluck. The children and I will go and find her.'

'I would have thought my military experience might be put to better use,' objected the toy soldier.

'What better use than to guard my uncle?' Fritz retorted. 'Only the most heroic of us could be trusted with such a job.'

Captain Pluck was immediately appeased. He stood to attention, indicating that his guard duties had already begun.

'I know my way around — we'll be back with her in no time,' Fritz reassured his uncle.

Von Gobstopper, a little shaky from the exertion of leaping to his feet, had no choice but to acquiesce to his nephew's instruction. Fritz affectionately draped a rug around the old man's knees.

'How will we find her?' Ernest asked.

'If she was part of the last round-up, we know exactly where to find her.'

CHAPTER FIFTEEN

Saved by the Bard

With a growing dread in their hearts, the children accompanied Fritz and Theo back to the basement. When they reached Hack Ward, they felt palpable relief at not finding Pascal in one of the narrow beds. They hoped this meant she was still in the arcade somewhere. But then they saw two Botchers scrubbing up at metal troughs, at the same time polishing off their glasses of whisky. The Botchers were in no apparent hurry and it took only seconds for Fritz to lead them all past as soundlessly as ghosts.

In the operating theatre, under a huge spotlight and buckled onto a trolley by a series of clasps and belts, lay an unconscious Pascal. Her cheeks were drained of their usual ruby colour and Milli shuddered to imagine what she'd been thinking when the anaesthetic was administered. A trolley bearing implements similar to those they had seen before was waiting beside the sleeping doll. A screen on the ceiling showed a Tempest Anomali design that detailed the proposed changes to the prima ballerina doll; the Botchers would only need to look up occasionally to follow her instructions. If they achieved only half of the suggestions outlined the post-surgery Pascal would be monstrous. She would have extra eyes in place of her dimples, her head would be shaved and covered with metal scales, and from her navel would hang electric wires that emitted a charge on touch. Army boots would be glued to her dainty feet so she wouldn't be able to dance a single step. The design bore Tempest Anomali's swirly signature and trademark bolt of lightning crossing the T.

A small needle attached to a massive syringe was inserted into the back of Pascal's hand. The sight of it made Theo emit a deep rumble of rage. With the greatest care, he withdrew the needle with his paw and flung it to the floor in disgust.

'Untie her,' he instructed gruffly, but before anyone could move the sound of footsteps came from just outside.

'Behind here!' cried Milli, grabbing Ernest and pulling him down behind a trolley piled with sheets. Theo and Fritz followed, and they all huddled there together, pulling the sheets around them in a disorderly fashion to conceal their presence. They saw the Botchers' feet, swathed in ruched netting, enter the room. The men staggered a little, which they seemed to find rather amusing, and shared a joke about steady hands not being a requirement in their current positions.

They half-heartedly turned their attention to the ballerina doll strapped to the table, still decked in her opening night finery. One of the Botchers reached for a pair of nail scissors and began snipping roughly at the delicate bodice of her gown.

'This one was hard work,' he commented. 'Kept kicking and squealing. Even bit a golly's hand at one point. Beautiful, though.'

His partner gave a malicious chuckle. 'I enjoy working on the pretty ones,' he said. 'I like to see their faces when the bandages come off. What's this?'

Ernest felt his heart stop, but then saw that it was only the disconnected syringe that had drawn the Botcher's attention. The man picked it up from the floor with a puzzled look.

'Must have knocked it out in her sleep,' said his partner. 'They do that sometimes, jerk and jolt all over the place.'

The first doctor blew off any dust clinging to the hypodermic needle before re-inserting it.

'Better get started,' he said. 'The game starts at five. The Big Lugs against the Knobbly Knees — should be a good one. Will you look at this! These instruments haven't been cleaned since the last theatre. There's glue on these scissors. That's happened three times in a row now. I don't know about you, but with or without a licence to practise, I'm not putting up with this.'

'First things first,' said his partner. 'Open her up.'

'Not without sterile instruments — this is an insult!' The Botcher let out an exasperated sigh.

'Okay, I'll get a fresh lot. But lay off the grog while I'm gone.'

The remaining doctor moved to a metal cupboard and rummaged around inside, humming 'Raindrops on Roses', a popular musical theatre tune. A clatter indicated that the faulty air conditioning had just come on, and its buzzing allowed a hushed conference to take place behind the trolley.

'I say we tackle them,' hissed Theo, his teeth and fists clenched. The children had never seen him this riled.

'It's worth a try,' agreed Fritz. 'We'll distract them from the operation if nothing else.'

Milli thought it was a desperate plan and looked at Ernest for support.

'*All the world's a stage*,' he said cheerfully.

Theo and Fritz exchanged confused looks.

'Not now, Ernest,' said Milli crossly, wondering how he could be so insensitive at such a time.

'*All the world's a stage*,' he repeated doggedly, as if the words had a hidden meaning he expected them to divine. He decided to help them out. '*And men and women merely players …*'

'What's he babbling about?' growled Theo.

'He's quoting Shakespeare,' said Fritz, who, Milli observed, must be a cultured young man. 'I think he has a plan.'

Ernest's face broke into a wide grin and he nodded enthusiastically at Fritz. Then he put his finger to his lips, indicating they should wait for the other Botcher to return.

When he did, and the two men were unwrapping fresh instruments, Ernest cupped his hands around his mouth and began to speak in a floaty, far-away voice. His plan was inspired by the school production of *Macbeth*. In the event that an understudy may be required, Ernest had decided to learn every character's lines as well as his own.

'*It will have blood, they say: blood will have blood!*'

A troubled silence followed. Neither Botcher trusted his own ears. With their professional reputations already in tatters in the outside world, neither doctor was prepared to add hearing voices to their list of shortcomings.

'What was that?' one of them finally hissed.

Again Ernest called out: '*Turn, hell-hound, turn!*' Their semi-inebriated state played havoc with their reasoning skills. The Botchers seemed shaken. A small chisel clattered noisily to the floor.

'Is it a trick?' asked one.

'A ghost more like,' whimpered the other. 'It's the ghost of the doll.'

'Don't be a damn fool!' his colleague said. 'There's no such thing as ghosts.'

'You keep going then,' spluttered the superstitious one. 'I'm reading it as an omen of what's in store if we touch this doll.'

'*He shall live a man forbid,*' Ernest moaned. He was beginning to enjoy himself now.

Both Botchers stood paralysed, unable to continue. Theo decided to get in on the act.

'I am one who perished under your knife years ago,' he intoned in a low, gloomy voice. 'I haunt these corridors at night looking for retribution.'

'I am Raggedy Ann,' sang out Milli. 'Woe befall those who gave me a tail.'

'I am the lion whose roar you stole,' Fritz contributed. 'But my teeth and claws are intact.'

'Set Pascal free,' they chimed in unison, 'and your punishment may be less severe. Set her free … set her free!'

'I want out!' cried one of the doctors, sounding like a frightened child. 'I knew this was a bad idea the moment I got here. It's not natural. Remember what happened to Victor Frankenstein?'

'I'm with you,' declared the other. 'I even see them in my sleep now. They stand there staring at me and pointing to their scars. It's horrible.'

In their rush to leave the theatre, the Botchers knocked over the tray of implements and brought it crashing to the ground. As the doctors fled like maniacs down the corridor, their arms flailing, the rescue party scrambled from its hiding place and Pascal was gently lifted into Theo's waiting arms.

'Let's get out of here before anyone comes to check on their progress,' Fritz said.

They ran in what they thought was the direction of the basement steps, but the passageways all looked identical and they found themselves

223

temporarily lost. Fritz skidded to a halt and glanced around to get his bearings.

'We're in the west wing,' he muttered. 'Come on, it's this way.'

They rounded a corner and their faces filled with new panic. Two more Botchers, gowned and wearing caps on their heads, were heading their way.

'Intruders! Catch them!' one called out, and Milli recognised Dr Savage's voice as well as his thick sideburns.

Fritz looked from the Botchers to Theo and the others, then back again, and decided on a course of action. He let out a blood-curdling war cry and ran at the men, an action that surprised the Botchers and stopped them in their tracks for a moment. Milli and Ernest followed Fritz, and together they leapt and kicked and jumped on the men's backs, causing enough mayhem to allow Theo to duck through the mêlée to safety, carrying the sleeping Pascal in his arms. They'd almost worn the Botchers down when reinforcements arrived, drawn by the noise, and the children and Fritz were wrestled to the ground.

With their arms pinned behind their backs, Ernest, Milli and Fritz were led by red-faced and dishevelled Botchers to their common room. The doctors mopped their brows and poured each other stiff drinks whilst someone alerted Tempest Anomali. Everyone knew she'd arrived when the doors were kicked open by a metal-tipped boot.

Everything about Tempest Anomali suggested turbulence, Milli thought, from the strands of hair falling over her face like black twigs to the crocheted shawl slipping from her sharp shoulders. Something she hadn't noticed before was that Tempest had a wandering eye. It was something she usually managed to control but when she became riled or over-excited, as she certainly was now, the eye wandered off so far that only the white could be seen. It made her look quite deranged. She pinned the children and Fritz with her good eye and her upper lip did not stop quivering with pent-up emotion.

'What have we here?' She stalked towards them, too tall for real gracefulness. 'Hopeless children and a renegade employee!'

'They abducted a patient from theatre,' a Botcher informed her.

'Who was on duty?'

'According to the roster, Spleen and Bunion, but they're nowhere to be found.'

'In hiding, no doubt, hoping it'll all blow over,' scoffed Tempest. 'How did they get to theatre anyway — in wheelchairs?'

No one felt sure enough of Tempest's reactions to attempt laughter. Instead they looked fixedly at particular flecks in the grey floor, hoping she'd soon dismiss them. It didn't help that she was carrying a silver-tipped cane; she had been known, when in one of her furies, to attack them with whatever she happened to be carrying at the time.

'And where, pray, is the patient?' she continued.

'I'm afraid she escaped,' replied one of the Botchers sheepishly.

'Escaped? How?'

'She was assisted by a teddy bear.'

'Do I look like an idiot?' she screamed. 'Are you asking me to believe you were outwitted by a soft toy?'

'He was a particularly large soft toy,' said Dr Savage.

Tempest Anomali was about to bring her cane crashing down on the surgeon's head when he blurted out something that stopped her.

'I heard him speak to the doll.'

At this, the look in Tempest's eyes grew even wilder and she threw back her head and let out a piercing scream. It sounded just like a cat whose tail has been trodden on.

'*Spoke*? Can this be true?' she spat out. 'Have Dr Illustrious paged immediately! This is an emergency.'

Milli and Ernest felt their skin prickle at the mention of a Dr Illustrious. It was just like the feeling you get before the onset of an allergic reaction. Tempest Anomali's words had confirmed what the children had suspected for some time now. They had last seen Lord Aldor being carried in pieces off the battlefield by his ally Federico Lampo. *This is not the end* was his final threat. *You will see me again.* Had Lord Aldor returned to fulfil his promise? Were they about to come face to face with him yet again?

**

The door swung open a second time and two nasty-looking characters pushed into the common room. They were Bertha Slurp and Alistair Phony-Phitch and together they made up the marketing division of Von Gobstopper's Toy Arcade. The pair were also Tempest's fiercest rivals and competed jealously with her for Dr Illustrious's attention. Somehow they had got wind of trouble and had come to gloat. They sincerely hoped it would mean a reprimand for Tempest — something they wanted to see for themselves.

'What's going on here, Tempest?' Phony-Phitch taunted. 'It is imperative that the arcade's public image remains untarnished.'

Bertha Slurp's eyes twinkled maliciously. 'I don't expect the doctor's gunna be too pleased.'

Bertha had the face and shoulders of a bull terrier. She was short and stocky with calves like tree trunks and ankles that bulged over too-tight shoes. She wore a wool skirt and a twinset in pale lavender. Her stringy grey hair was pulled back from her face in a tight ponytail and her skin was blotchy underneath poorly applied foundation. There were broken capillaries either side of her coarse nose. Slurp was a nickname she'd carried from school, no doubt acquired due to her eating habits as well as her abnormally large tongue, which her mouth wasn't quite able to house. Some of it was always hanging out, like a forgotten piece of washing on the clothesline. As a consequence, she had constant pools of saliva at the corners of her mouth, which she had to slurp back into her throat if she tried to say too many sentences at once.

Alistair Phony-Phitch, on the other hand, was the sort of person who can slather on charm like sunscreen. He wasn't unattractive, with limp dishwater blond hair, a blobby nose and a set of tiny perfect teeth. His hooded blue eyes drank in everything and gave nothing back. He wasn't oily or unwashed, but nevertheless had a slippery quality that made him generally disliked amongst the medical staff. He wore an olive-green velour jacket and an open-necked shirt with a cravat. He would have had no trouble working as a double agent: he was intrigued by intrigue and felt loyalty to no one.

'You'd better let us go,' warned Milli. 'If we're not home soon, our parents will be sending out a search party.'

'The doctor'll know 'ow to deal with you,' said Bertha with a nasty giggle. She turned to the Botchers. ''Ave youse let Illustrious know they're 'ere? What's keepin' 'im, I wonder?'

'Silence, Slurp, I give the orders around here,' said Tempest cattily. She cast a nervous look towards the door and gave a short burst of hysterical laughter, then turned stony-faced again.

Time passed and the tension mounted, then the sound of running feet put everyone on alert. A lab assistant wearing safety goggles and holding a blowtorch burst into the room. 'He's on his way!' he cried. 'Dr Illustrious is coming.'

The announcement sent the entire room into a frenzy. Some of the Botchers opened their clipboards and pointed things out to each other in an effort to look productive. Others ran about gathering empty coffee mugs and plumping up the cushions on the couches. Everyone smoothed down their clothes, tucked away stray hairs and stood as straight as boards,

230

like primary-school children awaiting a visit from the headmaster.

Tempest Anomali gripped the children's shoulders very hard and leaned over them. 'Tricks won't help you now,' she hissed.

Dr Illustrious must indeed have been important because his arrival was preceded by no less than three bodyguards. First came a brutish-looking man with a solid tank-like body and a face so featureless that at first glance it looked like a flesh-coloured blob. It didn't take a genius to guess that he was there for his strength rather than what was between his ears. The man's clone filed into the room after him, followed by a third identical figure. They all had earrings in one ear, folded arms over their black shirts and eyes hidden behind reflective sunglasses. Milli thought they looked ridiculous, like thugs from a gangster movie, but their grim expressions left no doubt that they took their jobs very seriously indeed. Their names were Mince, Wince and Vince.

When Dr Illustrious finally made his entrance, the people in the room turned as silent as a church congregation and lowered their eyes respectfully. All except for Tempest Anomali, who threw herself onto the ground, arms stretched heavenward in a fervent kind of worship.

Lord Aldor had certainly changed since the momentous battle at the gates of Mirth. They hardly recognised the mad magician they had come to know and dread. Somehow he had reinvented himself and adopted a completely new identity — that of the sleek and urbane Dr Illustrious.

CHAPTER SIXTEEN

A Wicked Conglomerate

Dr Illustrious had very short silver hair, so short it was just a mat of sparkling bristles on his head. His eyes, the colour of polished river stones, gleamed and their pupils were abnormally large. They expanded ever further, like a stain, when he sighted Milli and Ernest. The long beard had disappeared, replaced by a trimmed moustache. He wore an elegant black suit, a spotty tie and his shoes were wrapped in the white muslin covers surgeons wear when they enter an operating theatre. Only one of his hands was bare; the other was encased in a fawn glove. The index finger of the gloved hand was missing, leaving a peculiar-looking gap, as if he had been taken apart and put back together in a hurry. Ernest noticed that one of his ears was also missing, the coral pink ear canal gruesomely exposed.

When Dr Illustrious threw his head back to examine the children more closely, they saw his lips were wrinkled like the skin on decaying fruit. His own skin was pulled taut over his bones but sagged beneath his eyes like two used teabags. The whites of his eyes (what remained of them) glowed like torches in his shrunken face. The disturbing calm that had always characterised him, abandoning him only temporarily during their last encounter, had returned. He regarded the children coolly, showing neither hatred nor triumph, merely an expression of emptiness. It made them think of a walking corpse.

Tempest Anomali spoke, still in her kneeling position. 'We did not wish to disturb you, Master,' she cried, the words oozing from her mouth like syrup, 'but we have discovered something that had to be brought to your attention.'

Dr Illustrious stroked Tempest's head, as if she were a household pet. 'Yes,' he said softly.

234

'You were right to summon me. I prefer dealing with old enemies myself.' His lips curled back over sharp teeth.

Tempest puffed up with self-importance as she sat on her knees and wagged a thin finger in the direction of the children. She seemed to be having difficulty keeping her dodgy eye from rolling back in her head, so overcome was she with devotion.

'They were caught interfering with our plans,' she told her master, 'and they were not working alone.'

Dr Illustrious stared at the children with his glassy eyes. Without the long beard and hair ornaments, he appeared smaller and thinner and, if possible, even more chilling. He glided over to Milli and Ernest. They met his frozen stare, refusing to be cowed. He placed a gloved finger beneath Milli's chin and lifted her face. She recoiled at his touch and a wave coursed through her body like icy water.

'Older but no wiser, I see,' he teased softly. He withdrew his finger and Milli was left feeling as if the intense cold had burnt a hole right through her skin. Dr Illustrious made a disapproving sound with his tongue. 'You were hoping to surprise me, I think. I'm sorry to disappoint you but I have known of your presence since you arrived.' His politeness set their nerves on edge.

'We knew you had to be at the bottom of all this,' said Milli, with a show of boldness she did not feel.

'Sometimes you act every bit the child that you are,' said Dr Illustrious with a smile. 'I am disappointed in you two. Getting yourselves caught so soon rather spoils the fun.'

Tempest Anomali couldn't control herself. 'What are you going to do with them, Master?' she asked in a tone of girlish excitement. 'Bury them, barbecue them or blast them into space?' She twisted a lock of her hair compulsively as she spoke.

'Lovely ideas, thank you, Tempest, but I have yet to decide. They may be put to some use before they are disposed of.'

'Of course.' Tempest nodded in deference to his higher thinking.

'Let me at 'em!' was Bertha Slurp's simple solution. She snarled so enthusiastically that she had to be restrained by Alistair Phony-Phitch.

'Why not let me drown them in my charm?' he proposed.

'Drowning's our job,' said Mince, stepping forward and speaking on behalf of his brothers.

'Shut up, you fools,' said Dr Illustrious in his most snappish voice since his arrival. He returned his attention to the children and resumed his courteous tone. 'How remiss of me not to introduce my esteemed team of specialists,' he said. 'I don't believe you've met Doctors Clive Cranium, Hideous Blunt, Pancretia Juice, Matron Spate, Nurse Tong and the famous Dr Pesto Proboscis. They are responsible for the medical miracles performed here.'

'Oh, right,' whined Alistair Phony-Phitch. 'Administration is always undervalued.'

Dr Illustrious ignored him. 'Of course, their work would not be possible without the generous funding of our benefactor, Gustav Von Gobstopper.'

At this the entire room erupted into laughter. Tempest Anomali held her sides; Alistair Phony-Phitch laughed so hard he had to use his cravat to dab at his eyes; and the thuggish trio slapped their thighs and pretended they'd understood the joke.

'Whatever you're planning, you won't get away with it,' said Fritz, incensed by the ridiculing of his uncle. 'The Von Gobstopper family is known and loved worldwide.'

'Your family pride is touching,' said Dr Illustrious dismissively, 'but useless.' He leaned in towards Fritz and continued in a whisper: 'When we have finished with him, Von Gobstopper too will be disposed of, like the refuse that he is.'

The veins in Fritz's neck throbbed and he lunged at Dr Illustrious. He was intercepted by Mince and Wince who shoved him back against the wall. Dr Illustrious looked mildly entertained.

'Have you learned so little from our encounters, children? Have you not seen that strength is rewarded and innocence punished? The golliwogs soon realised that — they work for me now.'

'Only because you did something to them!' shouted Milli.

'Now, now,' Dr Illustrious chided. 'A tweak here and there never hurt anybody. We all have a dark side — all I did was tap into theirs.'

'This is the saddest you've ever been,' taunted Milli, 'vandalising toys to make yourself feel powerful.'

'Oh, but you are quite wrong. It isn't power that motivates me these days. I've moved on from that to something infinitely more satisfying. Can you guess what it might be?' Dr Illustrious allowed the silence to expand before answering his own question. 'Revenge, of course. Did you think I would endure public humiliation without trying to settle the score?'

'You think you'll get revenge on us by ruining toys?' Ernest asked in disbelief.

'Not exactly. Allow me to show you the method behind the madness. As a fellow scientist, I think you'll appreciate this.'

Dr Illustrious glided from the room, indicating that Tempest and the trio of bodyguards should follow. The thugs gripped Fritz and the children roughly by the arms and hauled them off down the passage too.

Milli noticed that as soon as Dr Illustrious had left the room, the doctors snapped shut their clipboards in relief and resumed their conversations about snow sports and home renovations.

There was a smell like burning rubber throughout the tunnel-like passages. Milli and Ernest tried to take in as much as they could of their route for future reference but were hampered by the low-flying bats that kept swooping over their heads. They could hear the hum of machinery and clattering from the pipes that ran along the length of the ceiling. In the walls were mausoleum-like compartments and Milli wondered what they contained. At one point they heard shuffling sounds and saw that it came from the padded slippers of the surgeons who scuttled through the passageways like rats in a maze. Their groups parted respectfully on sighting Dr Illustrious, allowing him room to pass.

Finally Dr Illustrious stopped at a large wooden door heavy with giant hinges and bolts. There was tinsel draped above the lintel, the

240

handles were in the shape of antlers and a Christmas wreath hung from one. Most baffling of all were the words written in Christmas lights:

Santa's Workshop

The children and Fritz looked at one another, puzzled. What possible connection could there be between the jolly man in a red suit whose arrival was eagerly awaited at the end of each year by children across the globe and the deadly Dr Illustrious?

Dr Illustrious flung open the door to reveal a large room filled with the smell of burning. A great open furnace with a stone hearth stood in one corner, and inside it was a huge Christmas tree, blazing so fiercely the children had to shield their eyes from the heat. The tree was reduced to a pile of ash so quickly they knew it must be an enchanted fire. A group of small trolls appeared hauling another tree, which they threw in to reignite the blaze. They were hideous-looking creatures with flattened faces and tufts of coarse black hair sprouting from their nostrils and chins. Their ears were bat-like, they had swollen potbellies, and their arms and legs were lumpy with queer-shaped growths. Their green eyes were bright and round, and they grumbled and cursed as they worked. The children realised they were a horrible distortion of Santa's helpers.

In the middle of the room was a half-finished version of what looked like Santa's sleigh. Trolls clambered over it like insects, applying paint and lacquer where needed, stitching the seats and polishing the headlamps. A group of six reindeer were harnessed to the sleigh, but they weren't the sort of reindeer children fantasise about seeing the night before Christmas. These are usually gentle-faced and friendly-looking. The reindeer in Santa's Workshop had matted coats, their antlers appeared to have been sharpened into spikes and their eyes were large, bloodshot and mad-looking. The biggest of them, presumably the much celebrated Rudolph, was the grumpiest of all. His red nose was badly inflamed from a cold and flies buzzed around his ears, which were moth-eaten like a wool coat that has been too long in storage.

The trolls not tending the fire or preparing the sleigh were busy packing toys, their actions synchronised like those of workers on an assembly line. On the floor was a huge pile of striped gift boxes. Troll one handed a box to troll two, who randomly selected a mutant toy from the rows on the benches and packed it snugly between layers of tissue paper. Troll three sealed the box and decorated it with ribbon. Troll four (white-haired and wearing spectacles) dipped his nib into an inkwell and wrote names on tags, which troll five attached to the gifts. The children immediately recognised the names on the gift tags — it appeared that every child in Drabville was to receive one of these horrible gifts.

Some younger trolls scampered around in aprons, cleaning up, and they sang a little song as they worked:

> *What do you want for Christmas, little girl,*
> *   little boy?*
> *Fancy a scarred, slashed and mutilated toy?*
> *A clockwork sprouting giant moths?*
> *A teddy with a nasty cough?*

A dolly impaled with a metal probe?
A Barbie with no earlobes?
Put in your orders, come on, don't be shy,
Thoughtful Saint Nick will always comply!

As they sang, the children noticed that the trolls' teeth had started to rot from a diet made up entirely of mince pies. Their dental hygiene was not helped by their aversion to toothpaste. The children could not know this but the trolls had a taste only for sugary preparations and used only liquid liquorice as a mouth wash.

In another corner of the workshop, two trolls were testing Christmas crackers that, when pulled apart, spurted a greenish liquid that smelled of rotten eggs. Others were decorating a charred tree, not with shiny baubles but with bits of old bone and balls of fur. The bells grunted instead of tinkling, and the tinsel was thick with thorns. The worst thing was the ornament that crowned the lifeless tree. In my house (as I'm sure is the case in yours) we have a gold star or an angel at the pinnacle of our tree, although one year there was a digression from this tradition in order to proudly display an angel made from a toilet roll and cotton wool, constructed by me at pre-school. Perched at the top of the trolls' Christmas tree was a stuffed bat, its wings spread like an umbrella.

'Precious, isn't it?' purred Tempest Anomali. 'Christmas redefined.'

Milli and Ernest were horrified by the sights before them, but they didn't understand their purpose. Dr Illustrious had succeeded in ruining many of Von Gobstopper's beautiful creations, the children of Drabville would be taken aback to receive his hateful gifts, and Von Gobstopper's name might be forever blackened, but parents could easily buy their children toys from other companies like Harrowsmith or Fluffball. So what had Dr Illustrious really achieved?

'This won't change anything,' Ernest said smugly. 'Christmas isn't even about presents.'

Some trolls who overheard him glanced at each other and rubbed their blotchy hands together. 'Wrong!' they jeered. 'This Christmas is *all* about presents.' A dark look from Dr Illustrious silenced them.

'Little Pustule, you are too cocky,' the transformed wizard told Ernest with calm

245

disgust. 'Do you think I would go to so much trouble without an inspired plan? But like everyone else, you will have to wait to see it in glorious action.' He paused to scratch his chin thoughtfully. 'On the other hand, you are special people with whom I have forged a strong bond. I would be honoured if you would come along for the ride.'

'They're not going anywhere with you, you demented monster,' Fritz warned.

'Silence!' snarled Dr Illustrious. 'I have little patience for heroic types.' He signalled to Tempest, who in turn snapped directions at a troll.

'Let's give them a sneak preview,' she said.

The troll snapped off a prickly finger from one of the cacti plants in the shape of human hands that grew from the walls, and sniggering, tossed it on the fire. The children and Fritz sprang back as a wall of flames erupted inside the grate. The room was plunged into darkness and the furnace formed a kind of blazing stage. Figures moved inside the flames, as they might on a television screen with faulty reception. The figures seemed to be set on fast-forward and three scenes appeared in rapid succession.

The first was what seemed to be a playroom — the floor was littered with building blocks and board games. A small boy was sitting cross-legged in front of a large painted toy box. He stuck his hand inside, in search of something, then withdrew it instantly, shrieking and waving his arm. The children could see that a toy dinosaur had sunk its razor-sharp teeth into the boy's hand. A second scene began to take shape. This time it showed a cosy kitchen where a child was sprinkling sugar on her bowl of porridge whilst her mother busied herself making a pot of tea. On the table sat a rag doll with thinning wool hair and one eye suspended from a thread. The girl dropped her spoon and as she bent to pick it up, the doll withdrew a tube labelled *Ground Glass* from her apron pocket and emptied the contents into the porridge. The final scene was a brother and sister fast asleep in their nursery. A bear, who had been lying on the chest of drawers face down, got up and tiptoed over to the sleeping children. He withdrew a pouch from beneath his waistcoat and, with an evil leer, released a family of hairy-legged poisonous spiders under the children's bedcovers.

A feeling of helplessness washed over Milli and Ernest as they stood transfixed by the scenes of betrayal they had just witnessed. Fritz's face was burning with fury.

'As you see,' gloated Dr Illustrious, 'traitors in your very midst. An ingenious plan, if I say so myself. Now, get out of my sight!'

Led by Tempest, the trolls roughly escorted Ernest, Milli and Fritz to a narrow underground cell. It was dank and airless and they felt like animals trapped in a cage. It was difficult to breathe and the only sound was that of water dripping from a pipe nearby.

'No one takes on Dr Illustrious and wins. You of all people should know that,' said Tempest in triumph, and marched off.

The three captives sank onto the damp floor and contemplated a future that seemed entirely without hope.

'I can't believe it's happened again,' Ernest moaned quietly. 'Is it ever going to be over?'

'At least this time we were better prepared,' said Milli.

'You think so?' said Ernest. 'Then how come we're in here?'

Fritz slapped the walls in frustration. He was not accustomed to being rendered useless and didn't know how to react. The physical strength he had relied on up until now was inadequate in this situation. He paced the cell, clenching and unclenching his fists and glaring into space.

Several hours passed. Milli and Ernest wondered what time it was and what their parents would think when they discovered the children's second disappearance in as many days. Their legs grew cramped and their bodies stiff. They tried to sleep, but couldn't doze off no matter how hard they tried. A wave of panic surfaced every time they almost succeeded in relaxing; they were afraid of what might creep up on them and take them by surprise.

Dr Illustrious had mentioned them accompanying him on a ride. If the journey he had in mind was a real one, where was he planning on taking them?

CHAPTER SEVENTEEN

Loyal's Sacrifice

n an attempt to distract Milli and Ernest, as well as calm his own frayed nerves, Fritz withdrew from his pocket a Spinning Rascal — a gadget you and I know better as a Spinning Top. This was a variation on the original design — once it started spinning it went looking for grumpy adults to trip up. There is nothing that exasperates adults more than stumbling over toys children have failed to pack up, and Spinning Rascals have been known to lie in wait for parents to come home before spinning into a frenzy right at their feet and sending them sprawling. The children took turns whirling the Spinning

Rascal, which spun randomly around the cell in search of adults lurking in corners. They wished they could use it to trip up Tempest or Dr Illustrious long enough to make a getaway.

It seemed an eternity before a muffled thumping finally broke the silence. They listened intently, and there it was again, this time a little closer. When a troll cracking a whip did not appear, they dared to believe that in one form or another help was coming. The noise had now become more of a clack than a thump, and whoever was making it seemed to stop from time to time, as if to get their bearings. All three prisoners held their breath in anticipation, and soon the familiar face of Loyal the rocking horse appeared outside the bars of their cell.

Loyal peered in at the children who had to keep from crying out in relief.

'Loyal, I knew you were coming,' said Milli, throwing her arms around his neck through the bars. The hug was rather awkward, but his slightly coarse coat felt reassuring under her fingers.

251

'Thank goodness you're all right,' Loyal said to all three of them. 'You had us worried for a while.'

'We're OK,' Milli replied, but then looked around miserably. 'Apart from being trapped with no way out.'

In reply Loyal turned side on and they spied a rope hanging in a neat coil from his saddle.

'Loyal, you're a legend!' cried Ernest, which caused the modest rocking horse to flush with pleasure.

Fritz lost no time in tying one end of the rope to the cell door and Loyal clamped the other end tightly between teeth that looked as tough as granite. The rocking horse gave the rope such a heave that the cell door was dislodged. A second wrench and it was pulled clean off its hinges and rattled to the ground. They waited some moments to check if the noise had alerted the trolls, and relaxed when they heard nothing.

'How's Pascal?' Ernest remembered to ask as they scrambled out.

'A little shaken, and more than a little embarrassed at the trouble she has caused, but otherwise fine,' Loyal replied matter-of-factly.

'I might add that she has had a dream and found her true vocation.'

'That being?' prompted Fritz.

'She intends to hang up her slippers and train as a nurse.'

Despite their precarious circumstances the children had to laugh at the impetuousness of the ballerina doll they had come to love.

'What have you managed to find out?' the rocking horse asked.

'Dr Illustrious is planning to ruin Christmas!' Milli blurted out.

'He has some mad revenge plan that involves delivering mutant toys to the town's children,' Ernest said.

'But there's more to it than that,' added Fritz. 'Dr Illustrious isn't going to all this effort just to give the children a *fright*. He could just walk down the street to do that. These toys are dangerous and could cause harm.'

Loyal's brown eyes clouded as he digested this information. 'You can explain everything later,' he said. 'Let's get you to safety first.'

But before they could move, there came the menacing sound of heels clicking on a hard surface. They all froze on the spot, their hearts hammering in their chests. Discovery was inevitable.

The black-clad figure of Tempest Anomali rounded the corner to confront them. She had changed into a medieval gown with fluted sleeves. Her wild hair had been scooped up into a muddle on the top of her head and was held in place by combs that bore a sinister resemblance to ravens' claws. Around her white throat she wore a necklace made of tiny speckled eggs and black eyeliner lent her eyes a feline look. She was still carrying her metal-tipped cane. When she saw the door of the cell had been yanked off and spied the rocking horse with the rope end still in his mouth, her chalky face paled even further with anger. She moved towards Loyal with the stealth of a panther.

'Stay back,' Loyal warned in a low voice. He positioned himself in front of Milli and Ernest.

But Tempest, used to dealing with toys that were weak and submissive, only laughed. She tried to shoulder past him, but Loyal stood his ground. A momentary look of confusion crossed

Tempest's face. She recovered quickly and lunged at Milli and Ernest, but Loyal's rockers blocked her path. The two collided and Tempest tumbled to the floor. Loyal cautiously retreated, but still remained protectively positioned in front of the bewildered children.

'Let them be,' he warned.

Milli and Ernest saw Tempest's hands start to shake and her nostrils flare with rage. The expression they saw on Fritz's face told them their fears were not without foundation. He was watching Tempest warily, his arms and shoulders tense.

Tempest kicked out violently but missed her aim, and broke her heel on one of Loyal's rockers. The shiny black wood was left scratched and indented.

Fritz pushed Milli and Ernest away from Tempest. 'Run!' he said urgently.

The children looked confused and didn't move.

'Don't wait — go now!'

But Milli and Ernest were cemented to the floor. They wanted to turn and run until their lungs ached, but they couldn't move a single muscle — not whilst Tempest was closing in on Loyal again.

Her second kick was powerful and sent the wooden horse crashing into the wall. Tempest smirked with pleasure at her own strength and raised her disdainful eyebrows before zeroing in on the children. She seized Milli in an iron grip, but Loyal heaved himself to his feet with a grunt and he threw himself at Tempest. She reeled back and let go of Milli's wrist.

Loyal, too, implored the children to run. 'Didn't you hear Fritz?' he said. 'Go!'

'We're not leaving you,' Milli cried, and the rocking horse brayed with frustration.

He opened his mouth to speak again, but Tempest clutched at a handful of his mane and used it to drag herself up. Loyal whinnied in pain and nipped her hand. She let out an enraged howl and clutched it, bleeding, to her chest.

'The others need your help!' Loyal panted. 'I can handle her alone!' His breath was knocked out of him as Tempest lashed wildly at him with her cane.

Fritz could stand it no longer and went to Loyal's aid, grabbing both of Tempest's arms and pinning them behind her back. Despite her rage, the curator was no match for Fritz's strength, but at that moment five figures rounded the corner, alerted by the noise of the scuffle. The children recognised the three bodyguards followed closely by Bertha Slurp and Alistair Phony-Phitch.

Mince threw Fritz to the floor, whilst Bertha restrained Milli and Ernest in a chokehold. There was nothing further to be done. All three of them were prisoners and Loyal was surrounded.

Despite the cruel faces leering down at him, the rocking horse showed no sign of fear. For a split second he caught Milli's eye and seemed to pass on to her a message of hope. Loyal's eyes were as warm as ever and Milli felt strangely comforted. The feeling was immediately replaced by a terrible numbness as the sound of splitting timber filled the air. Loyal lay in a broken heap in the corner. His rockers had been snapped, rendering him immobile, and he could only snap his teeth helplessly at his attackers.

With her confidence restored, Tempest approached the rocking horse with menace in her eye. The children watched in stunned horror as a spearhead shot from the tip of her cane. She plunged it coolly and ruthlessly into the horse's side, then stood back looking rather pleased with her efforts.

With a superhuman strength fuelled by grief, Milli, Ernest and Fritz wrenched themselves free of their captors and rushed to Loyal's side. The horse let out a feeble moan and struggled to keep his eyes open.

'Hang on, Loyal,' begged Fritz, his eyes luminous with tears. 'Uncle Gustav will mend you, as good as new.'

'Dear Fritz,' faltered Loyal, 'do not fail us now.' There was a shuddering exhalation as the rocking horse breathed his last.

Tempest and the bodyguards prodded him with their feet.

'Keep away from him!' Milli cried, her face tear-streaked as she tried to shield Loyal with her arms.

What happened next the children would later recall only as a blur. The world had taken on a foggy, dream-like quality. They felt the grip of strong arms propelling them forward, they smelled a combination of tobacco and alcohol that told them they were back in the common room, but it was as if they had detached from their bodies and were watching themselves from a height. It was only from her dry, raw throat that Milli suspected she had been screaming at some point.

All of Milli's vitality had ebbed out of her and it took a great deal of concentration just to curl up in a ball on one of the green vinyl couches. She was dimly aware of Fritz's hand on her back and his tear-stained face looking down at her.

All three listened with complete indifference to the babble of voices around them, deliberating on what was to be their fate. Alistair Phony-Phitch eventually sidled up to them with a smarmy announcement.

'Dr Illustrious has invited you to be the guests of honour at our Christmas party tonight.'

'You're joking, right?' snarled Fritz. 'What makes you think we want anything to do with brutes like you!'

Alistair Phony-Phitch looked mildly offended. 'Watch who you're calling brutes,' he said. 'This job is a stepping stone for me on the ladder of success. Besides, nobody has ever knocked back an invitation from the doctor before.'

The children were issued with Santa hats and forced to attend what could only be described as a parody of a Christmas party. It was held in the canteen, where the plastic chairs had been draped with black tinsel. A large wreath of thorns sat as a centrepiece on the long table. The baubles and bells strung up across the room were also black, creating a morbid feel. In place of balloons, inflated surgical gloves had been tied in small bunches from the ceiling fan. The Botchers finally looked cheerful as, for them, it marked the close of a long year. They were looking forward to spending time with their families and not having to practise their peculiar brand of surgery for at least a month. Dr Illustrious and Tempest were there, sipping cumquat champagne from test-tube glasses. Tempest wore a lock of horsehair, the colour of crème brûlée, around her neck as a pendant.

Eggnog was being served and there were bedpans full of Christmas fare — roast turkey, fruitcake, plum pudding and mince pies. Dr Illustrious ate nothing; Tempest nibbled reluctantly on some turkey slices.

Tempest called everyone's attention by banging her cane on the table, and announced that Dr Illustrious was about to make a speech.

'Before we farewell each other and head off to different destinations, there are some acknowledgments that need to be made,' the doctor said. 'Firstly, I must extend my thanks to all the arcade staff for their commitment and service in what, at times, have been less than ideal circumstances. You will all find a Christmas bonus in your pay envelopes.'

Cheers broke out at this point and the Botchers exchanged self-congratulatory nods. In their eyes, the bonuses were well and truly overdue.

Dr Illustrious waited for the last cheer to die down. 'Secondly,' he said, 'heartfelt thanks must go to our director and chief designer, Ms Tempest Anomali. No one here could deny that without her warped vision, our great work would

261

not have been possible. I'd like to present her now with a small token of our esteem.'

One of the trolls materialised from the kitchen carrying a huge bunch of blackened twigs. Tempest could not have looked more pleased had she been presented with diamonds from Tiffany's. The Botchers applauded half-heartedly.

'I look forward to seeing you all again, refreshed and ready for new projects,' continued Dr Illustrious. 'We will, of course, be operating out of our new premises by the new year, directions to which will be issued to you via snake mail towards the end of next month. Make sure to keep your compasses handy.' Dr Illustrious chuckled as if he'd just told a hilarious joke. 'And now there appears to be nothing more to say other than *Happy Holidays and enjoy a well-earned break!*'

Unrestrained applause arose from the Botchers, especially those planning to hand in their resignations immediately after collecting their pay packets. Some Botchers hung up their lab coats and headed for the door, but others stayed chatting and refilling their glasses from the bottles of French cognac carried around on trays by trolls whose wide grins bore witness to the fact that they too were partaking liberally.

Dr Illustrious was suddenly behind the children. 'Do you know what day it is today?' he breathed into their necks. It made their skin prickle in discomfort. 'It's Christmas Eve,' he said. 'Time for that ride you were promised.'

Milli and Ernest felt as if they had resurfaced from the bottom of a very deep well. How could it be Christmas Eve already? It wasn't possible. When they had returned on Loyal's back to the arcade, there had been days until Christmas. Could time have passed so quickly?

Milli's thoughts spun instantly towards Peppercorn Place and her family. What must they be thinking? It was Christmas and their youngest daughter had gone missing for the second time that year. Had they pinned her stocking up on the mantelpiece or had they put it away in a drawer and given up on her altogether? She didn't think she could blame them if they had.

Ernest thought of his family too, but also mourned the loss of something else. Christmas

263

was supposed to be a time when the spirit of cheerfulness pervaded everything — the decorations, the music, the feasts, the gifts were supposed to fill you with irrepressible happiness. It made you want to show kindness to others — *spreading the Christmas cheer* they called it. People looked forward to Christmas for months. He didn't think it fair that Dr Illustrious could just waltz in and take it all away. So much effort would go to waste and so many children would be bitterly disappointed. He had felt himself losing his own Christmas cheer of late, thinking of it as more a chore than a celebration. He didn't like this change in himself and certainly wouldn't wish it on others. He thought of his younger siblings and how much Christmas meant to them.

Dr Illustrious's voice broke into his thoughts. He sounded impatient. 'Are you ready? The sleigh is waiting for us. Of course, you may stay here if you prefer. If you *want* to spend Christmas locked in a cell.' His eyes narrowed deviously. 'I *was* planning to drop you home to your parents,' he said, 'after our little journey.'

'We'll all go,' said Fritz.

'I'm afraid you are needed here,' said Dr Illustrious with a cold smile. 'Tempest cannot be without her assistant.'

He gave the children a mock bow. 'You must excuse me whilst I change into more appropriate attire for tonight's journey.' He turned to his entourage. 'Meet me on the roof in ten minutes.'

Part IV

A Stronger Power

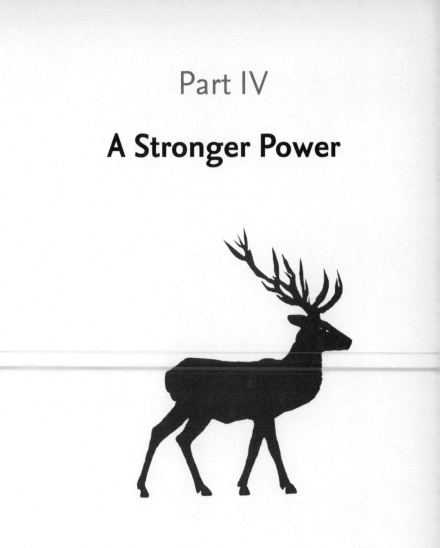

CHAPTER EIGHTEEN

Sleigh Ride

About half an hour later, the door opened and Tempest Anomali beckoned them with a long finger. 'Now the fun begins,' she said, rubbing her hands together.

As Milli walked alongside the designer she found herself imagining horrible things, like forcing Tempest to undergo the surgery she had inflicted upon the toys, pulling her hair out or trampling her with an army of dolls and teddy bears. Although she knew it wasn't right to think such hateful things about anyone (no matter what their crime), Milli couldn't help feeling that Tempest deserved it. She tried to ease the anger that was bubbling furiously in her chest but this only seemed to aggravate it further. She wanted Tempest punished for what she had done and it took an enormous amount of self-control not to rush at her and knock her down on the spot. But Milli knew that if she had any hope of seeing her family again and foiling Dr Illustrious's plans, she would need to be clear-headed. For Loyal's sake, she would think rather than react. That is what he would have wanted of her.

Tempest led the children to the top level of the arcade, up a narrow staircase and out onto the roof. Waiting for them there was Santa's sleigh. It gleamed cherry red and gold in the moonlight, symmetrical black patterns lacquered on its side. Fairy lights studded its edges and bells and lanterns hung off its elegantly curved back. Milli realised at once that anyone seeing it from below would never guess that its driver had such sinister intentions. The seats were made of soft, warm leather and two fur jackets waited for the children, to protect them from the falling snow. Milli was reminded of stories her history teacher at St Erudite's had told them about prisoners receiving kind hospitality before being led to the gallows.

The nine mangy reindeer stood in two neat rows at the front of the sleigh, holly wound around their antlers. They snorted and pawed the ground, eager to get going. The children saw Rudolph's inflamed nose glowing like a beacon in the darkness. The sleigh was filled with bulging sacks brimming with brightly wrapped presents. In the middle of it all sat Dr Illustrious, looking nothing like the fat and jolly Father Christmas he was meant to be impersonating. First of all, he was too thin. His red coat trimmed with white fur hung off him limply and there weren't enough holes in his belt to fasten it securely around his middle. His false beard was lopsided and his hat flopped over his eyes. The only thing that fitted properly were his black shoes. He looked gangly and awkward, but Milli supposed that from a distance no one would see through his disguise.

'What will you do if you run into the real Santa on your way?' she asked him spitefully. 'He's not going to be too happy about this.'

Dr Illustrious laughed cruelly. 'Myths are usually harmless,' he said.

'What about those who believe in them?' Milli countered.

'Be silent, you insolent girl, and follow instructions. Get in!'

Reluctantly, the children climbed up, took their places and put on the fur coats.

'Ho, ho, ho!' the magician cried triumphantly as he lashed his whip. The reindeer looked alarmed and broke into a trot. Another crack of the whip and they began to run.

Ernest gripped Milli's hand as the edge of the roof approached. 'Are you sure this is going to work?' he called out in a panic, but Rudolph had already leapt from the edge, followed by the next two reindeer.

As the sleigh slid from the rooftop it dipped alarmingly and the children found themselves sitting in midair for a split second. Then they were flying above the snow-capped trees and Milli thought that if their ride hadn't been imbued with such sinister intent it would have been almost magical.

As the reindeer did not travel in a straight line, but rather swerved and swooped all over the place, they felt rather like they were on a rollercoaster ride. They were soon flying over the rooftops of Drabville. The houses were decorated with fairy lights and holly wreaths adorned the doors. Snowmen had been constructed in front gardens and tinsel wrapped around letterboxes. The whole town was immersed in the Christmas spirit and totally unaware of what was in store for them.

Dr Illustrious steered the reindeer towards a terracotta roof some ten metres away. With a gentle clop of hoofs they landed. Milli and Ernest recognised the house as that of their dear friend Gummy Grumbleguts and his family. Milli knew for a fact that Gummy's little sister, Gummola, had been counting down the days until Christmas for months now. The little girl was hoping for a doll to replace the one she had accidentally dropped in the river at the Midsummer Festival. Milli shivered to think of what would happen when she opened her gift in the morning.

Dr Illustrious rummaged around in a sack labelled with various house numbers and withdrew an oblong box wrapped in striped green paper with a shiny silver bow tied around

273

its middle. Milli had to admit that it looked appealing. Dr Illustrious withdrew a larger box for Gummy, wrapped in paper decorated with bright pink cakes and puddings. Lugging the gifts under one arm, he moved towards the chimney and stopped to fasten a hook to the top of it. Laughing under his breath, he unravelled a rope and tested his weight on it. He cast the children a sly glance before cocking one leg over the side of the chimney and disappearing from view.

Before Ernest could say a word, Milli had jumped from the sleigh, unlatched the hook and dropped the rope down the chimney after the magician.

'Milli!' Ernest hissed. 'What are you doing? He'll kill us!'

'We have to do something,' Milli hit back. 'We've sat like lumps for long enough.'

Much as Milli must be applauded for her brave effort to stop him, Dr Illustrious had been prepared for such an attempt and was hardly even delayed by it. Milli was just jiggling the reins and urging the reindeer forward when a soot-blackened hand rose up from the mouth of the chimney. It was followed by shoulders, a waist and finally the skull-like face that had become so familiar. Milli noticed a swirling blue mist at his feet and cursed herself for being foolish. She had forgotten that he had powers beyond that of an ordinary man. Dr Illustrious looked even more deranged than before (if that was possible), perhaps due to the soot now smudged under his eyes and the scrape down his left cheek. The children shrank back as he drifted towards them, and Milli dropped the reins as if they were hot coals.

Dr Illustrious resumed his place at the head of the sleigh then glanced at them over his shoulder.

'Rope slipped, did it?' he said with a smirk. 'Dear me, I must be more careful.'

The journey continued in the same way, the sleigh stopping at each house for Dr Illustrious to deliver his fatal gifts. He was only ever gone a few moments but the children knew how much damage he caused in that short time. Once he returned holding a glass of milk and a note and wearing an expression of disgust.

'What do you call this?' He smirked at Milli and Ernest. 'A bicycle, a board game and a kitten all in exchange for a glass of milk. Humans continue to astound me.' He tore the note into little pieces, and let the glass of milk smash on the lawn below, before pulling out of his pocket a silver flask of strong-smelling liquid which he gulped hastily.

In the magician's brief absences, the children tried in vain to find various means of escape or sabotage. They considered jumping from the roof, before realising they would most likely break their legs. They thought about blocking up the chimney with sacks to prevent him climbing back out, but found that the sacks were stuck to the sleigh by enchantment. When they tried to encourage the reindeer to take flight, they refused to budge and made such a racket that the children didn't dare a second attempt. At one stage in mid-flight they were spotted by a family on their way home from late-night celebrations. Milli and Ernest waved desperately at them and called out, but they only squealed and waved back in delight.

'Ho, ho, ho!' Dr Illustrious cried out. 'Merry Christmas, my friends!' And the sleigh sped away, leaving the family stunned to have finally glimpsed the real Santa Claus at last rather than just some tubby old fellow in the department store.

As the hours rolled by, the children couldn't keep their eyes open and soon fell asleep leaning against one another. They woke with a jolt just as daylight was beginning to break. True to his word (for once), Dr Illustrious delivered them safe and sound to their own homes.

'Someone's going to stop you,' Milli cried. 'You won't deceive the town again. You'll never succeed!'

The magician laughed as he lashed the beasts and drove the sleigh high above the chimney tops. He looked down at her.

'It seems I already have,' he called out as the sleigh sped into the dawn.

'Merry Christmas!'

Milli let herself into her house and stumbled down the hallway, flicking on lights and calling out to her parents as she went. Her unexpected arrival brought Stench barking wildly from his basket. He didn't calm down when he recognised Milli, but instead began to lollop playfully around her ankles, licking her hands. Stench had missed Milli these past few days. His excitement caused her to trip up and graze her knee on the carpet but she hardly even noticed. A bedroom door was suddenly flung open and there stood her parents, bleary-eyed and wearing dressing gowns. Rosie ran forward, scooped Milli into her arms and held her tight. Milli buried her face in her mother's shoulder and breathed in her familiar floral scent. For a moment all the outside dangers that had been plaguing her seemed to fade into a blur.

But Milli knew she couldn't give in to the comfort of home just yet, tempting as it was. She detached herself from her mother and, ignoring the volley of questions being fired in her direction, led her parents to the kitchen.

She waited for her family to sit themselves around the table with frothy mugs of cocoa before launching into an explanation of what was happening at Von Gobstopper's Arcade. She told them about Theo, the leader of the Resistance, the dainty Pascal and her narrow escape from the Botchers, the bold yet diminutive Captain Pluck, and the heroic and good-looking apprentice named Fritz Braun. She described the distressing experiments being conducted in the underground laboratories and, in a choked voice, related the fate of Loyal the rocking horse. When she had finished, she looked hopefully at her parents. She wished she had sought their advice before now, but she had been too confident in her own abilities. It was a relief to be finally handing the responsibility over to someone else — as long as it wasn't too late.

'The other parents need to be warned,' said Mr Klompet without hesitation.

'Yes, but there isn't time,' Rosie replied. 'By now every family in Drabville will be on their way to Carols in the Square.'

It was a long-established tradition in Drabville for the townsfolk to gather very early on Christmas morning to sing carols and enjoy a lavish breakfast of crumpets, pancakes and hot chocolate. It was also customary for somebody's obliging father to dress up as Santa and hand out the presents to the children. There was a countdown, at the end of which all the children tore open their gifts. The town choristers sang some more carols and everyone drank eggnog before heading home for their private celebrations.

The Klompet family bundled into their coats and climbed into Mr Klompet's delivery van with its insignia of a steaming pie and the words *Klompet's Breads and Pastries* on its side. Milli was surprised to see her older sister, Dorkus, beside her. Dorkus's hands were plunged in her pockets and she looked uncomfortable at being so far from the security of the house. But there was also a look of determination on her face that Milli and her parents had not seen there before.

'It's OK, Dork,' Mr Klompet said to his elder daughter, 'you don't have to come. We'll sort it out and tell you all about it when we get back.'

Dorkus shook her head like a wilful child. 'Move over,' she said to Milli. 'I'm coming.'

Milli was so proud of her sister at that moment that she wanted to give her a crushing hug, but she thought better of it. She didn't want Dorkus to become self-conscious and change her mind.

***

The Klompet van made a quick detour into Bauble Lane, where they found a desolate Ernest sitting on the front steps of his house.

'What are you doing out here?' asked Milli.

'I've been disowned and disinherited,' he replied forlornly. 'During our absence, my mother's blood pressure hit an all-time high.'

This seemed rather dramatic behaviour, Milli thought, for such a reserved family. She wondered whether there might be a touch of Mediterranean blood somewhere down the line that Ernest was unaware of.

'Don't be silly,' said Milli's mother. 'Everyone's just very upset.'

She rang the doorbell. The usually vague Mr Perriclof answered, looking red-faced and agitated.

'I can't believe you have the temerity to turn up at my home,' he exploded. 'Hasn't your daughter done enough damage? Poor Roberta hasn't been able to leave her bed in days!'

'Oh, shush!' said Rosie crossly. 'We don't have time to explain now but our children haven't

281

done anything wrong. In fact, they've put themselves at risk in order to save others.'

Rosie gave a burbled summary of what had happened, and when she'd finished Mr Perriclof looked mortified and gave his son an apologetic smile.

'What are we standing here for?' he exclaimed, piling into the back seat with the others. 'There's no time to lose.'

CHAPTER NINETEEN

The Countdown

he delivery van sped along Drabville's cobbled streets, narrowly avoiding bins and lampposts. No one inside spoke; words seemed unnecessary. All eyes were glued to the road ahead. Finally the town square came into view and they could make out the small stage that had been rigged up for the choir, now singing 'White Christmas', a famous Christmas melody. The spectators stood in clusters, rugged up in coats, mittens and hats. Some grandparents sat in folding chairs and poured hot drinks from thermos flasks. The children were clearly restless, trying to listen respectfully to the singing, but their eyes kept wandering over to the pile of presents at the back of the stage. As if by magic, they had all selected the gift with the brightest paper and special name tag, believing it would contain the biggest surprise. The van pulled up and its occupants tore out just as the countdown was beginning. Mr Hapless, Harietta's father, was almost unrecognisable in his costume, until he tripped over the microphone cord and lost his Santa hat, which gave him away entirely.

The children were lifted onto the stage where they congregated in a large huddle, each clutching a present to his or her chest. Their faces were bright with excitement. They were nearly blinded by the camera flashes as doting parents recorded the event.

'Wait!' Milli shouted over the din of band instruments.

But nobody heard her or even glanced in her direction.

'Nine, eight, seven, six,' cried the townsfolk, joining in with Santa's countdown and clapping their hands in time to the music.

'Don't open them!' yelled Ernest. 'You don't know what's inside!'

'Four, three …'

'They can't hear us!'

'Two, ONE!'

From there everything happened rather quickly. We all know what children are like when unwrapping gifts — there is no delicacy or thought of saving the expensive paper for re-use. If you think back to your own experience with gifts, I'm sure you will remember tearing off the wrapping paper and flinging it to the floor, impatient to end the suspense and feast your eyes on the contents within.

Before Milli and Ernest had reached the stage, its surface was awash with wrapping paper, ribbons and discarded cards, their messages far too predictable to bother reading. But as the presents were revealed, each child fell silent. They stared into the boxes, their eyes wide. The parents, who had been expecting looks of elation, were confused.

Finally, a voice broke the silence. It belonged to a little girl called Polly Brook whose collar was always starched and pigtails perfectly matched.

'Yuck!' she cried, dropping her present to the ground. 'It's horrid!'

The gift landed with a heavy thud and suddenly everyone saw its repugnance. What had once been a sweet-faced doll with blonde plaits and an upturned nose had been transformed into something quite repellent. Her eye sockets were empty, their rims painted a lurid red. Long, hairy fingers sprouted from her gums and her hair had been replaced by coiled rubber snakes. She wore overalls and out of the top pocket poked the curved tip of what could only be a knife.

The other children took their toys from their boxes and held them out to their parents in protest. It took the adults some time to register what was happening and they were slow to react. Some of the mothers gasped and put their hands over their mouths, horrified by the sight of the mangled toys. Some grandparents made tut-tutting sounds, believing they were witnessing someone's macabre idea of a joke. But once the initial shock wore off, people began to panic. The children on stage started to wail, many kicking away the offensive objects. Some pushed their way to the edge of the stage hoping to rejoin their parents.

Nobody had gone far when a sound from above startled everyone. The familiar words rang out over the square — words that filled Milli and Ernest with dread. 'Ho, ho, ho!' cried a voice and the tinkling of bells filled the square. Children and adults alike forgot their shock and instead exclaimed in wonder, craning their necks to catch a glimpse of the lacquered red sleigh hovering above them like a vision. So entranced were they at seeing the myth of Santa Claus come to life that many forgot all about the strange gifts and broke into a cheer. They waved at the sleigh, perhaps hoping Santa had arrived to rectify his mistake.

'Don't trust him!' Milli yelled, as she and Ernest rushed onto the stage. 'He's not Santa!'

But for the second time that morning nobody heard her desperate plea. They were all too preoccupied clapping and watching the reindeer perform graceful manoeuvres in the sky. What they didn't realise was that the reindeer weren't being entertaining; in fact, they were preparing themselves for something quite sinister. They began to rock back and forth and suddenly jets of fire spurted from their nostrils towards the stage where the children were standing. Parents screamed and siblings shielded one another but the flames were enchanted and had only one purpose: to form an impenetrable ring of fire around the children. They were now trapped within the flames, inaccessible to their parents.

If you think being imprisoned inside a ring of fire with a collection of mutant toys and a deranged villain in a Santa suit flying overhead sounds bad, imagine the terror the children felt when Dr Illustrious drew a black oblong object from his coat pocket and pointed it directly at the toys littering the stage.

At first the children thought it was a weapon and cowered, but when Santa started clumsily pressing buttons they realised it was a remote control. The buttons activated small microchips planted deep within each toy. Before the children's eyes, the pile of mutant toys wriggled and came to life.

Little paws, claws and hands reached over the rims of cardboard boxes and the toys scrabbled their way out. Another flick of Dr Illustrious's remote control and they swivelled around until they were facing the startled children. They began to advance fixedly, with synchronised movements. In the bright sunlight their deformities were even more pronounced — they were a mass of contorted faces and clumsy bodies.

The children tried to back away but were trapped by the searing flames. Through the fiery barrier they could see their parents, their faces paralysed by shock as the toys closed in.

CHAPTER TWENTY

Love is Blind

Milli watched in horror as the toys fell into step like marching infantry. Some of them had fingernails as long and sharp as knives. Others carried small bottles that contained what she imagined to be poisons of the deadliest sort. Some drew weapons from their pockets or from the lacy hems of gowns. One thing was clear — each and every toy was intent on wreaking havoc of the worst kind and the trapped children had nothing but ribbon and crumpled wrapping paper to use in their defence.

'Papa!' cried one little child.

'Please, stop them!' cried another.

Some children were sobbing openly now, unconcerned with keeping up appearances. Several others called out to their parents, but the adults could do nothing except stand there helplessly, arms waving and mouths moving in silent panic.

The Drabville fire brigade arrived and tried frantically to extinguish the flames but they didn't respond to being doused with water. If anything, they seemed to leap even higher in devilish mockery. Some heroic firemen tried to brave the flames in their yellow heatproof suits, but found that the fire acted as a kind of force field and they could not get past it to help the children.

There was no time for logical thinking. All the children could do was band together on the stage, with the youngest at the back, and try to defend themselves. But as the toys were armed with all manner of weapons there seemed little chance that everyone would escape unharmed.

Ernest succeeded in kicking a doll into the fire and hoped he had destroyed her, but the doll re-emerged seconds later. Even though part of her plastic face was melting, making her look more ghoulish than before, she continued to advance with the army of toys.

As he hovered above in his sleigh, Dr Illustrious opened his arms and let out a peal of triumphant laughter. As he did so a harsh wind blew up around him, tearing off his disguise. First the red coat and wide belt were whipped away, followed by his pants, gloves and buckled shoes. Underneath was not the pitch black suit the children were accustomed to seeing Dr Illustrious wear, but long flowing robes. Finally, Dr Illustrious tore off his hat and beard revealing himself to the stunned onlookers. A collective gasp rose from the crowd when they saw him. He might be wearing his hair cropped short but there was no mistaking the hollow eyes and shrunken features. The children could not decide what to be more frightened of, the advancing army of evil toys or the skeletal figure of Lord Aldor glowering at them from the skies.

Lord Aldor's laughter lashed the crowd like a whip. Above the clamour rose the voice of one of the fathers, Bert Granger, a hulking dairy farmer who wasn't prepared to take what was happening without putting up a fight. He stepped forward with his clenched fists raised and eyes glowering.

'Whaddya want with our children?' he bellowed. ''Ave you not plagued us enough? For pity's sake, let them go.'

Lord Aldor peered curiously over the edge of the sleigh.

Bert Granger continued, 'If you 'ave a beef then take it up with us. What kind of coward are yer, to attack defenceless children!'

Others added their jeers but Lord Aldor's gaze was so unflinching he might have been a god on Mount Olympus looking down on the little clay people to see what they were up to. Looking up into Lord Aldor's face was like looking into an empty wasteland where it was lunacy to expect to see anything there other than desolation. Even Lord Aldor's mouth when he opened it to speak was as dry as a crater.

His voice filtered down to them. 'You look confused. Would you like to understand my motivation? The truth is, I hate every last Drabvillian to the core. You people reek of *cheerfulness, spirit, resilience* and I have grown tired of it. The very scent of you is like acid on my skin. This town was meant to be reduced to ruin years ago but you have somehow eluded my schemes. I tried to be fair but you scorned my generosity. I am here now to prove that you cannot resist my will — your lives are not your own! It is I who decides your fate! Your world will exist as I dictate, and I say there shall be no happiness, no music in the streets, no laughter. Only when I have achieved this shall I be at peace.'

With these final words, Lord Aldor pushed a button on his remote control and the toys crouched in readiness to strike.

'Attack,' he said coldly. 'Let them suffer as I have suffered! Let the hills ring with the echoes of their screams for years to come.'

The toys were close enough now that the children could see the imperfections in their stitching and the dried streaks of glue where weapons had been added to their bodies. Some children tried to remember their prayers, whilst others looked around desperately for something to stave off an attack.

Milli's mind went into overdrive trying to think of all the knowledge she had amassed during her short but event-filled life. Nothing of much use presented itself. She did know that when you are in the strangest of situations help can sometimes come from the least expected quarter. She ran through all that had happened since her and Ernest's first visit to the toy arcade and replayed every conversation in her head. As the thoughts raced through her mind she realised that perhaps the most important message had come from the toy she had treasured most. She could almost hear Loyal's gentle voice as if he were right there beside her: *Toys have been the allies of children for centuries. It would take something more extraordinary than an operation to change that.*

With the rocking horse's words echoing in her mind, Milli did something that many people might have considered rash, foolish or just plain dangerous. Taking everybody, including herself, by surprise, she stepped forward and scooped the nearest toy into her arms. It was a teddy bear, and no sooner had she embraced him than he dropped his pocket knife clumsily to the ground. She hugged him tight to her chest and whispered into his furry ear, her hands stroking his deformities and hideous scars. The bear seemed to go limp in her arms, all his aggression falling away, and the two stood melded together in the way children and their toys often interact.

The other toys came to a baffled halt.

Milli turned slowly to face the other children, who were staring at her in shock. The look on her face told them what they must do.

Ernest was first; having a penchant for girly toys, he hesitantly picked up a doll. Finn and Fennel, who were also stranded on the stage, wasted no time in following Ernest's example. When Milli looked around she saw their old comrades like Gummy Grumbleguts, Harietta Hapless, Horace Rugknuckle and Prudence Cackle were quickly following suit, each gathering a toy into their arms. Due to his size, Gummy thought it only fair that he get hold of two. In the space of a few moments, every child was embracing a toy, despite their scars and wrongly placed limbs. Their faces were horrifying, their bodies lumpy and uneven, but the children pushed away any fear they had and tried to think of these toys as old friends who had been neglected for some time and therefore deserved more of their attention. The children of Drabville held those poor misshapen toys and spoke to them in soothing tones until the mechanisms that had been planted in them to cause harm short-circuited and burnt out and every toy was simply content to be wanted.

It is a toy's nature to respond to the scent and touch of children. These are as familiar to toys as the scent and touch of our mothers is to us. The children could almost feel the hatred and resentment drain out of the toys. A strange sense of homecoming overwhelmed them all. And as it did, the wall of fire vanished, leaving only a ring of ash on the stage.

The adults stood speechless for a moment, watching their children. Then they ran forward like a wave, exclaiming in admiration and relief.

A sudden creak from above drew everyone's attention. Lord Aldor's sleigh was lurching from side to side as the reindeer struggled to keep it airborne. Milli wondered if it had been the menace of the toys that had kept it off the ground. With that dissolved, the sleigh was slowly but surely falling. It gave a last shudder before plunging towards the earth at an alarming speed. The townsfolk scattered, pulling their children well out of harm's way.

The impact of the collision when the sleigh connected with solid ground made the earth tremor and kicked up a huge cloud of dust. When it cleared and people could see and breathe properly again, the bent figure of Lord Aldor was visible clambering from the wreckage. The wizard now found himself surrounded, with not an ally in sight. The reindeer had somehow recovered from their fall and scrambled away into the night.

The townsfolk drew nearer, no longer fearful of his powers nor enraged by what he had attempted to do. Instead, they felt only pity for this shrunken old man who had wanted to rob Drabville of Christmas. A citizen nearby reached out a hand to support Lord Aldor as he staggered a little, shaky on his feet. For a brief moment, hesitation crossed the magician's face, as if somewhere in the deepest part of him there was a small hankering for acceptance. Then his expression darkened again. Lord Aldor may have been exhausted but he was not about to allow himself to be humiliated in front of a crowd of mortals. If he did, his reputation would be dust. He gathered all of his remaining strength and concentrated hard on levitating out of their reach. He succeeded in raising himself a few inches above the ground before his body collapsed under him, like a tree that has withered from the inside.

A sudden shout from above had every face turning towards the sky. There was the silver rocket from the arcade that the second group of children had ridden in. At the controls, dressed in a silver spacesuit, her hair in sleek black coils, was the curator, Ms Tempest Anomali. She landed the rocket at a safe distance and emerged shrieking at the top of her lungs.

'I'm coming, Master!' She swatted away the crowd with her hands as if they were flies. 'Get back! Don't you dare touch him with your filthy hands!'

Tempest Anomali supported Lord Aldor to the rocket, looking excited to have her mentor and master entirely dependent on her for the first time. Once she had him comfortably settled, she bared her teeth and hissed at the stunned crowd before climbing in herself and taking the controls.

'They're getting away,' Ernest said in despair.

And for a moment it really did seem as though Lord Aldor and Tempest were about to escape without any comeuppance — until another figure hobbled into the town square, aided by a young man with a rather formal air. Milli and Ernest at once recognised Gustav Von Gobstopper and his nephew, Fritz Braun.

Von Gobstopper clutched a lacquered music box at which he seemed to be directing some kind of incantation. Had he gone mad, the children wondered. Had the stress of all he had endured sent him off the rails? But Von Gobstopper looked more focused and sure of himself than the last time they had seen him.

He opened the lid of the box a fraction and a streak of blue fire shot out. It circled the square once and then darted between trees and startled townsfolk. Finally it disappeared inside an ancient elm. The huge tree began to glow, shafts of blue light spinning from its branches in all directions. Then out stepped a woman with soft fair hair and blue robes that seemed to flow around her like water. A halo of light surrounded her entire body.

'The Blue Fairy,' whispered Milli.

'She's too late,' said Ernest. 'They're about to escape.'

But it wasn't too late.

From the folds of her robe, the fairy drew a wand in the shape of a twisted black twig and pointed it serenely at Tempest Anomali.

Tempest looked genuinely alarmed for the first time and raised both hands as if to shield herself. She tried to cower behind Lord Aldor, but he was intent on avoiding the wand himself and, with an unceremonious shove, jettisoned Tempest from the rocket. She landed on the ground in a surprised heap. Scrambling to her feet, she pleaded with Lord Aldor for assistance. As she waved her hands at him, something odd happened: her foot was suddenly where her hand should have been, and she was waving around her boot. Tempest watched in horror as the foot encased in its black studded boot began to blur. She blinked hard, hoping it was a delusion brought on by stress, but her foot continued to fade until it disappeared completely! She was left hopping ridiculously on one leg. The next thing to go were her hands and ears. The Blue Fairy moved her wand a fraction in various directions and Tempest continued to fade away piece by piece, until there was nothing left of her but a shred of silver fabric fluttering in the wind.

With a strangled cry, Lord Aldor jerked the rocket's controls violently and it jerked upwards. The crowd's final vision of Lord Aldor was of an old man with his mouth hanging slightly open, his eyes crazed with the knowledge of impending defeat and his body slumped as if every vestige of energy had left him. Even at his weakest moment Lord Aldor had never looked like this.

The rocket darted behind some clouds pursued by a flying column of blue. When the rocket came into view again it was swaddled in blue light. The light grew brighter and swirled around the rocket at such a speed that soon the light and rocket merged into a single blur. A spectacular explosion followed which saw the rocket catapulted through the sky in chunks. All that remained of its inhabitant was a rain of ash that floated softly down to earth.

Moments later the Blue Fairy was standing calmly by Von Gobstopper's side. The crowd saw but could not hear the words they exchanged before the Blue Fairy herself vanished from sight. For some time after she had left them the trees remained tinged with blue and the air seemed to resonate with a stirring power.

CHAPTER TWENTY-ONE

The Best-kept Secret

An affectionate reunion between parents and children followed, with much squeezing of cheeks and ruffling of hair. It went on for some time, until Milli climbed onto the stage and called for everybody's attention. The crowd looked up at her with a mixture of curiosity and suspicion.

'Don't celebrate yet!' she said into the microphone. 'There are still lots of toys trapped in the arcade. Lord Aldor may be gone, but he's left a lot of problems behind. Mr Von Gobstopper and his nephew need our help.'

'And whose fault is it that Lord Aldor came

back?' called out one parent, gripping her son's shoulder tightly.

'It was you he wanted, but instead he went after *our* children,' yelled another.

This unleashed a volley of accusations, which flew through the air like arrows. Milli flinched involuntarily.

Ernest scrambled up to join her, looking indignant. 'How can you all be so STUPID?' he demanded. 'Milli and I have only ever tried to protect this town. Would you rather we had done nothing and let Aldor carry out his vicious plan?'

There was silence for a moment as everyone considered this.

'Lord Aldor returned the first time to seek revenge on us because we rescued the shadows of Drabville and foiled his plan,' Ernest went on. 'Or have you forgotten that? Milli and I could have stayed living in luxury and left you all to live as robots, which would have been much easier — but we didn't. Not that it makes any difference to you lot. You still hold *us* responsible.'

'He's right,' piped up a small voice. It belonged to Pippa Squidge, one of the younger children who had been taken to Battalion Minor. It was only due to Milli's encouragement that she had survived. 'How can you be so blind?' she demanded. 'If it wasn't for Milli and Ernest, Lord Aldor would have sold us all at the market in the Conjurors' Realm, and who knows where we'd be now. You should be giving them a big reward, not getting cross with them.' She folded her arms and wrinkled her nose as she'd seen adults do when something displeased them. 'I am very disappointed in you all.'

Hearing these truths from one so small took the townsfolk by surprise and they were speechless for some time as they contemplated what had been said. The adults were used to using such words themselves in order to keep the children in check and did not like this sudden role-reversal. They felt quite ashamed of themselves. Then the most unexpected person stepped forward to speak. Usually it was such adults as Mrs Klompet, Mr Mulberry or Mr Percival Bow who took on the public speaking challenges, or at least someone who was a member of the Custodians of Concord. Nobody expected to hear from the person who now came forward.

'The child is right, for heaven's sake!' exclaimed Mr Perriclof. 'It'll do no good standing about like stunned rabbits. If there are toys in distress, then let us rescue them — we can't simply leave them there. Let us go now before any further damage is caused. I do believe the children have suffered enough!'

Whether it was the quality of Mr Perriclof's speech or the shock of actually hearing him speak, I'm not sure, but his words spurred the townsfolk into action. They took no weapons with them, just headed towards the arcade as a large group.

As Milli expected, the doctors, assistants and administrators had packed up their belongings and gone. They had not, however, had time to empty the laboratories.

The children were made to stay on the ground floor whilst the adults gently removed the toys from their hospital beds and transported them to the new temp orary Toy Hospital, which the Custodians of Concord opened on the spot in the Town Hall. Lots of volunteers wrote their names on a large sheet of paper, all eager to tend to the wounded toys. There would be plenty of jobs for everyone, Rosie Klompet assured the anxious townsfolk. They would need nurses and craftsmen and people to find the toys loving homes once they had fully recovered.

Nothing mobilises a town like a worthy cause, and this was the most sensible and worthwhile Drabville had been involved in for a long time.

Together, Milli, Ernest, Fritz and Von Gobstopper went to find Theo and the others, who were still in their underground hideaway.

'Don't tell us!' cried a distressed Pascal. 'Don't tell us what he has done!'

'It's okay!' Ernest said. 'We have good news. It's over.'

When they finished describing what had happened, and Pascal saw that Fritz's usually stern face was flooded with relief and the rigidity in his shoulders had dissolved, she spun into a delighted pirouette.

Milli leaned against Fritz's shoulder. 'The arcade is yours again!' she said. 'I don't expect Lord Aldor will be resurfacing any time soon.'

Ernest turned to Von Gobstopper. 'I can't believe the magic you implanted in your toys was strong enough to defy the powers of someone as powerful as Lord Aldor,' he said. 'Which means ... you truly are the best toymaker in all the world!'

Gustav Von Gobstopper smiled and squeezed the children's hands in his. He beckoned Fritz to his side.

'Who knows how things might have gone without your help,' said the toymaker. 'You are, without a doubt, the bravest children I have ever encountered. I think, Fritz, some new toys will have to be created in their honour.'

'My uncle and I cannot thank you enough,' said Fritz solemnly. 'Your kindness will not be forgotten.'

'What will you do now?' asked Milli.

'I am looking forward to doing very little,' smiled Von Gobstopper. 'Fritz here is more than capable of continuing the family business. It's time for Fritz to show the world what he can do.'

Milli and Ernest were eager to get back to their families, but the toys felt they couldn't let this momentous occasion pass without saying a few words. Theo went first, blushing slightly under his fur.

'You children have certainly proved yourselves worthy on more than one occasion,' he said. 'I feel very honoured to have met you both.'

He untied the black bandana that he wore around his head and handed it to Milli. He untied another from around his neck for Ernest.

'You've earned this.' Next, Pascal trotted forward, her tutu quivering with excitement. She tugged on Ernest's trouser leg and demanded to be picked up. Standing on her tippy-toes on his palm, she reached up and kissed him on the cheek, then did the same to Milli.

'I knew we could rely on you,' she said. 'How frightening it must have been out there! Oh thank you, thank you! Who knows where we would all be now if it hadn't been for the two of you. Can I come and live with you, Milli? I could be your special doll. Don't take offence, Ernest, it's just that I know you have brothers and little boys tend to pull my hair.' She lowered her voice. 'A friend of mine had all her hair cut off by a bored child with a pair of scissors. I should feel much safer in a household where the majority of occupants are women.' And she gave an almighty twirl that lasted several minutes.

Then it was Captain Pluck's turn to come forward. 'You have done well, young master,' he said to Ernest, nodding his wooden head emphatically. He drew his little sword from its sheath and coughed to indicate that he would like to be lifted up level with Ernest's face. Ernest obliged and Captain Pluck solemnly tapped him on each shoulder, stretching a little in order to reach. 'Wear this golden tassel with pride; we are honoured to have you in our ranks. For your contribution so far, I thank you humbly. You have the heart of a lion inside the body of a rabbit.'

Ernest's face fell a little at this. He knew he wasn't a solidly built boy, like Horace Rugknuckle, but he was almost certain that *rabbit* was a slight exaggeration. He chose to ignore it, however, and accepted Pluck's offering graciously.

The toy soldier then bowed deeply to Milli.

'Little Miss Klompet, you have proved to us all that not only are you fair of face but as gallant as the most daring of soldiers. You looked evil in the eye and did not swoon or scream or run away. I doubted you and for that I am deeply sorry. Can you ever forgive me?'

'Of course I can, Captain,' Milli said with a smile. 'You needn't even ask.' She couldn't help chuckling to herself as she looked at the soldier's worried little face. 'You *are* the silliest soldier I've ever met in my life,' she said and hugged him affectionately.

'We are very grateful for all you've done,' said Theo. 'You've saved us all and we won't ever forget it.'

'Not quite all,' said Milli softly, her thoughts returning to the prison and a pair of puddle-brown eyes.

'Yes, he was the best sort of toy, one of a kind,' said Theo quietly. 'And he will never be forgotten.' He placed a paw on Milli's hand. 'Try to think of him as he would want to be remembered. Think of all the wise things he said, and how he loved Pascal. Remember the trust you placed in him and how he never let

312

you down. Remember how his saddle shone, for he was proud of that.'

Milli felt a tear roll down her cheek and plop onto the floor. She saw that Fritz's eyes were bright with tears as well.

'We won't forget you, Loyal,' she whispered, so quietly that nobody heard her. '*I* won't ever forget you — just as you didn't forget about us.'

She rubbed her eyes and took a deep breath. 'Come on, everyone, let's introduce you to our town.'

Rosie was very pleased to meet Fritz and Gustav Von Gobstopper. The poor inventor was quite overwhelmed with the attention he was receiving. Everybody wanted to talk to him or shake his hand or ask him how he felt about all that had happened. In the end, Rosie was forced to put an arm around his shoulder and steer him out of the path of eager townsfolk.

'Let the man rest for a while,' she said. 'He has been through an ordeal.' It was settled that Von Gobstopper and his nephew would stay at the Klompet household for the time being until

313

alternative accommodation was arranged for them.

'You are too kind to us,' said Fritz, as his uncle was too stunned to utter a word. 'We don't wish to impose.' Rosie soon dismissed any such talk with a lecture about the importance of fresh food and an early night.

'Your uncle is in no state to look after you and you are far too young to be living alone,' she said.

'I'm almost eighteen,' Fritz replied, standing very tall.

'Nonsense,' Rosie replied, straightening his collar. 'Come along now.'

As they gathered outside to walk home together through the snow, Pascal sat propped on Ernest's shoulder whilst Milli walked between Captain Pluck and Theo, holding the teddy bear's hand in her own.

Milli saw her mother and urged the others along to catch up with her. 'Mum, I'd like you to meet some special people,' she said. 'This is Theo, Pascal and Captain Pluck — they looked after us in the arcade.'

Rosie looked from the toys to her daughter

314

and smiled. 'That's lovely, sweetheart,' she said.

'How do you do, Mrs Klompet,' said Theo, speaking slowly in order to make a good impression. When Rosie made no reply, a perplexed Theo tried again. Again, there was no response.

'Don't be rude, Mum!' Milli scolded. 'Theo's talking to you.'

Rosie smiled at her daughter indulgently, glad that her imagination hadn't been diminished despite the horrors she'd recently witnessed.

'I'm sorry, I didn't hear him,' she said. 'What was it he said?'

Rosie made a pretence of listening intently, but was distracted by a group of other parents asking her a question.

Milli tugged on her mother's sleeve impatiently. 'Theo's waiting for an answer!'

Rosie frowned for a moment, then leaned towards the bear. Theo repeated his greeting, more forcefully this time, and directed it at all the adults. In fact, he repeated it many times before the truth became apparent. As hard as the adults listened, they couldn't hear a thing.

Writing *Von Gobstopper's Arcade*, the last book in the series, has been a different experience not only because it has required a superhuman juggling of time between study and writing, but also because I am bidding farewell to Milli and Ernest, who have been my faithful companions over the last few years.

I would like to extend my thanks to all the young readers who have taken the time to write to me expressing their enthusiasm for the series. Your letters have provided the inspiration to keep writing even in difficult times.

Thanks to bffls — Miffy, Liva and Nat for supporting me all the way. Your friendship is invaluable. Particular thanks to Jenny Church for being there to remind me that I am an author and therefore must act like one.

As always, thanks must go to the committed team at Harper Collins for their encouragement and understanding and a special thanks to Lisa

Berryman for her wisdom, level-headedness and for always giving the impression that she has all the time in the world to chat.

Thanks to all my teachers for being so accommodating and for those extensions of deadlines. Much appreciated!

Lastly, a huge thank you must go to my mother whose patience and love never seems to run out.

ADO
Book 3